Wendy Wilcox's Foolproof Get-Yourself-A-Husband Plan:

1. Make a list of all marriage-minded bachelors in town. If you're left with only eighty-year-old stamp collectors, go to step 2.

2. Ask Travis, the sexy guy next door, for help. You'll baby-sit his adorable little boy if he'll teach you how to entice a man.

3. Throw yourself into your lessons: Get close on the dance floor. Put your whole heart into that pretend kiss good-night.

4. Have your friends give you a glamorous makeover and really wow that commitment-shy neighbor.

5. Forget finding yourself a man on whom to use all those wiles. Because by now you've discovered that Travis is the *only* groom who'll do.

D0802649

Dear Reader,

Well, I'll be honest: I didn't know *what* to write about this month. Women grow up hearing about falling for "the boy next door," but apparently I've always lived in the wrong neighborhoods. And I've never turned to a dating book for advice, preferring to meet men via serendipity. Of course, most recently that's meant being "courted" (and I use the term loosely) by the hot-dog vendor near the train station. (What can I tell you? New York is a funny place.) So I think I'll skip the personal-experience stories this month and get right to the books. After all, they're what you *really* want to know about.

First up, our DADDY KNOWS LAST cross-line continuity series continues with Carolyn Zane's *How To Hook a Husband (and a Baby)*. Here's where that hunky bachelor neighbor makes his appearance. And I'll tell you, if this book were set in a real town, I'd be packing my bags right now, because this man more-or-less next door is a winner.

Then there's Samantha Carter's *Dateless in Dallas*. She hooks up two as-opposite-as-they-can-get reporters to research the advice in the year's hot dating book, and the results are explosive. Of course, they're not what anyone expected, either, but does that really matter when true love is in the air?

Have fun—and see you next month, when we'll be bringing you two more terrific Yours Truly titles, the books about unexpectedly meeting, dating...and marrying Mr. Right.

Leslie Wainger
Senior Editor and Editorial Coordinator

Please address questions and book requests to:
Silhouette Reader Service
U.S.: 3010 Walden Ave., P.O. Box 1325, Buffalo, NY 14269
Canadian: P.O. Box 609, Fort Erie, Ont. L2A 5X3

CAROLYN ZANE

How To Hook a Husband
(and a Baby)

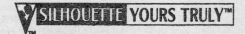

Published by Silhouette Books

America's Publisher of Contemporary Romance

If you purchased this book without a cover you should be aware that this book is stolen property. It was reported as "unsold and destroyed" to the publisher, and neither the author nor the publisher has received any payment for this "stripped book."

My thanks to the Aurora, Oregon, Post Office, especially Postmaster Dewain Winters and my mail carrier, Judy Pickett, for their many answers to my endless postal-related questions, and their sense of fun and enthusiasm for this project.

And, as always, thank you, Lord.

 SILHOUETTE BOOKS

ISBN 0-373-52029-8

HOW TO HOOK A HUSBAND (AND A BABY)

Copyright © 1996 by Harlequin Books S.A.

All rights reserved. Except for use in any review, the reproduction or utilization of this work in whole or in part in any form by any electronic, mechanical or other means, now known or hereafter invented, including xerography, photocopying and recording, or in any information storage or retrieval system, is forbidden without the written permission of the editorial office, Silhouette Books, 300 East 42nd Street, New York, NY 10017 U.S.A.

All characters in this book have no existence outside the imagination of the author and have no relation whatsoever to anyone bearing the same name or names. They are not even distantly inspired by any individual known or unknown to the author, and all incidents are pure invention.

This edition published by arrangement with Harlequin Books S.A.

® and TM are trademarks of Harlequin Books S.A., used under license. Trademarks indicated with ® are registered in the United States Patent and Trademark Office, the Canadian Trade Marks Office and in other countries.

Printed in U.S.A.

CAROLYN ZANE

When asked to participate in the DADDY KNOWS LAST cross-line continuity series, Carolyn Zane was thrilled. The opportunity to work with four other authors in a joint effort to breathe life into the fictional town of New Hope, Texas, has been one of the highlights of her career thus far.

Carolyn Zane lives with her husband, Matt, and baby daughter, Madeline, in the scenic, rolling countryside near Portland, Oregon's, Willamette River. Like Chevy Chase's character in the movie *Funny Farm*, Carolyn finally decided to trade in a decade of city dwelling and producing local television commercials for the quaint, country life of a novelist. And even though they have bitten off decidedly more than they can chew in the remodeling of their hundred-plus-year-old farmhouse, life is somewhat saner for her than for poor Chevy. The neighbors are friendly, the mail carrier actually stops at the box, and the dog, Bob Barker, sticks close to home.

Meet The Soon-To-Be Moms
of New Hope, Texas!

"I'll do anything to have a baby—even if it means
going to the sperm bank. Unless sexy cowboy
Jake Spencer is willing to be a daddy...the natural way."
—*Priscilla Barrington, hopeful mom-to-be.*

THE BABY NOTION
by Dixie Browning (Desire 7/96)

"I'm more than willing to help Mitch McCord take care
of the baby he found on his doorstep. After all, I've been
in love with that confirmed bachelor for years."
—*Jenny Stevens, maternal girl-next-door.*

BABY IN A BASKET
by Helen R. Myers (Romance 8/96)

"My soon-to-be ex-husband and I are soon-to-be
parents! Can our new arrivals also bless us with a
second chance at marriage?"
—*Valerie Kincaid, married new mom.*

MARRIED...WITH TWINS!
by Jennifer Mikels (Special Edition 9/96)

"I have vowed to be married by the time I turn thirty.
But the only man who interests me is single dad
Travis Donovan—and he doesn't know I'm
alive...yet!"
—*Wendy Wilcox,*
biological-clock-counting bachelorette.

HOW TO HOOK A HUSBAND (AND A BABY)
by Carolyn Zane (Yours Truly 10/96)

"Everybody wants me to name the father of my baby.
But I can't tell anyone—even the expectant daddy!"
—*Faith Harper, prim, proper—and very pregnant.*

DISCOVERED: DADDY
by Marilyn Pappano (Intimate Moments 11/96)

1

"**B**ang, bang! You're dead!"

Blowing on his imaginary pistol, Dustin Donovan shrieked with glee and crawled behind the couch as fast as his scraped-up, five-year-old knees could carry him.

Wendy Wilcox, his baby-sitter, next-door neighbor and dearest buddy affected her scariest voice. "Oh, no, I ain't, you biscuit-eatin' sidewinder. And I aim to come after ya, so ya better watch out," she shouted to him from behind the chair-and-blanket tent they'd built in the middle of her living room.

"No!" Dusty giggled, and from where Wendy sat she could hear him clumsily trying to disentangle his father's cowboy boots from her light linen drapes.

She sighed. No matter. The drapes could be cleaned. Nothing was more important to her than hearing the joy in her young neighbor's voice. He was only just now beginning to trust since his mother had left him and his father over three years ago.

In her peripheral vision she could see Dustin's sunny face peeking at her from behind the couch, his finger pointed in her direction, poised to shoot when the opportunity arose. He was such a beautiful child. Sweet, fair-haired, bright. The perfect combination of two striking parents.

Too bad neither of them had the sense the good Lord gave a rock. Shaking her head she blew a small puff of exasperation between her lips. Some people just didn't know when they were well-off. She'd give anything to have a marriage and a lovely little boy like Dusty.

But alas, she thought dramatically, so far it hadn't been in the cards for a fading wallflower such as herself.

Reaching into the breast pocket of her postal uniform for a handkerchief, she thrust it through the tent's opening and waved it at Dusty. "Hey, sagebrush breath," she called, and watched him drop back behind the arm of the couch, giggling all the while.

"What do you want, Dances With Polecats?" he asked suspiciously. It was his Indian name for her.

"I want to make a treaty with you, you crazy milk-mustached cowpuncher."

"No!" he screamed, and skedaddled across the living room to the relative safety of Wendy's armchair.

"There's chocolate milk in it for you."

Silence.

Wendy grinned and fought her way out of the lopsided tent. She knew how much he loved chocolate milk. "And I just rustled up some peanut butter and jelly rations. A tough customer like you must be pretty hungry." Again, silence. "Plus, I got us some chocolate chip cookies . . ."

Dusty groaned. "Okay," he agreed, standing to clump noisily across the floor where he settled down next to Wendy at her coffee table. Pushing his father's cowboy hat back on his silky, golden head, he propped his oversize boots out in front of him and pointed a grubby forefinger up at her. "But we're not done yet," he informed her, hoping that they could take up where they'd left off.

Wendy knew that as far as Dusty was concerned, they could play till the cows came home. He'd made it perfectly clear—on more than one occasion—that there was no place he'd rather be than at her side, pelting her with questions or playing a wild game of some kind. Preferably a game that involved running and shouting. The knowledge of his youthful devotion gladdened her heart. Somehow, having Dusty so nearby made the pain of not having a child of her own easier to bear.

Elbows propped on her coffee table, they dug into their sandwiches and chocolate milk, eating in a comfortable silence born of mutual trust and love. Wendy had moved into the small New Hope, Texas, neighborhood just before Dustin's mother had taken off, and ever since they'd met, he'd been her little shadow. She knew she was probably serving as some sort of substitute mother and it made her happy that she could focus her own unused maternal instincts on him.

Every so often, Dusty would mumble some cowboy-type phrase of appreciation for the good grub, and Wendy would nod in stoic Indian fashion. Tossing Dustin a small package of cookies, she reached for a pile of books and magazines that she'd bought at the New Hope bookstore earlier that day. She'd been so busy—what with Dustin's last-minute visit—she hadn't even had time to open them yet.

"Wendy?"

"Hmm?" she asked, flipping through the latest copy of *Metropolitan* magazine. The blurb on the cover blared, Do You Have What It Takes To Snare A Man? She shrugged. Obviously not, or she'd have done it by now. Perhaps this article would tell her what she'd been doing wrong.

"Where does chocolate milk come from?"

"Brown cows."

Dusty frowned thoughtfully, not sure if she was teasing. "Oh..."

Wendy winked at him, then allowed her gaze to wander back to the book titles that were stacked in front of her. *I'm Okay... We're All Okay, So Why Am I Still Single?* one book wondered. Another posed the question, *Are You Everybody's Friend, Nobody's Lover?* Yep, she sighed dramatically. That one hit the nail on the head. Then there was *How To Be Irresistible to Every Man, Every Time*. Gracious. She didn't want to be irresistible to every man. Just one. Nothing fancy. Just some likable lug to father a couple chubby little babies and mow the lawn once in a while. And bring her roses . . .

She ran her fingers over the title of her personal favorite, *How to Hook a Husband*. Hopefully, with all this advice from renowned specialists in their fields, she would have a man in no time. Because, if the article she'd found last week in the recycling bin down at the New Hope post office where she was postmistress held even a speck of truth, she had to do something drastic if she was ever going to have a family of her own.

Women over thirty—it had gloomily prophesied—had little or no chance of ever tying the knot. And Wendy was only a little more than a month away from the big Three-Oh.

The big Three-Oh-No.

Gadzooks! she thought, taking a big swig of her chocolate milk. She'd better get a move on. Time was running out.

Travis Donovan pulled to a stop in his driveway and cut the engine of his large, American-made, four-wheel-drive pickup. Thrusting his hands through his hair he absently studied the ceiling of his truck and inhaled the leftover scent of BambiAnn Howe's cloying perfume.

Damnation. That woman had more moves than a World Federation wrestler in training. Normally he'd have been more receptive to her vigorous and thoroughly creative maneuvers, but not tonight. Tonight he was beat. Wanted nothing more than to spend a few minutes wrestling with his five-year-old son, then off to dreamland. He'd had a grueling week and Friday had been a long time in coming. Thank heavens tomorrow was Saturday. Maybe he could persuade Dusty to sleep in. Yawning, he unhooked his seat belt and let it slide into its holder. Next week would be just as tiresome. Luckily, he'd managed to wrap up the remodel job on the New Hope Hotel, and would be able to start the job on the run-down post office come Monday.

His eyes strayed next door to Wendy's place. He'd have to tell her that he'd be over there on Monday. As postmistress she'd probably be glad to hear that. Hell, she'd been harping on him about needing more space in the back room for months now. No doubt she'd be thrilled with the addition that had been planned.

Travis and Wendy owned two homes that sat side by side at the back of one of New Hope's newest cul-de-sacs. Travis was especially proud of the houses on this street, as he and his crew had done the lion's share of the work on the project. Attractive, stylish middle-class houses with brick columns and arched windows, the houses were trendy, similar to a degree, yet nicely managed to reflect the owners' personalities.

Funny how Wendy's yard was adorned with so many flowers. He hadn't thought she'd be the type to go in for something so frivolous. His glance swept the shadows of her landscaping and landed on her picture window. Several lamps illuminated his son and Wendy as they gamboled around her disheveled living room. Travis grinned. Thank God for good old Wendy. He owed her big-time for all the evenings she'd taken care of Dusty recently. Which reminded him. He had to get on the stick about replacing his nanny. Ever since Kathy had left for college last month, he'd been up the creek without a sitter.

He watched as Dusty threw his arms around Wendy's legs and hung on, dragging along behind her as she made her way to the kitchen, then back to the living room. She was a good egg, that Wendy. Maybe she wasn't all that good-looking, but she was pretty cool with his boy. Salt of the earth. The kid practically idolized her. Maybe he'd pull out all the stops on that remodel for her. Build her some fancy shelves or something.

Hunching thoughtfully over his steering wheel, Travis watched the two at play. Yep, she was nice enough, but personally, he couldn't see the dazzling attraction his son had for her. For a moment he allowed his eyes to follow her as she moved around the room. She was no bigger than a young boy, really. Far too thin for his taste and—the breast man that he was—she lacked the main ingredient to capture his attention for any length of time. He smirked to himself as thoughts of the voluptuous BambiAnn jiggled and bounced briefly through his mind. Squinting at Wendy, he figured that she was probably just about as different from BambiAnn as a woman could be.

Wendy's mousy brown hair was ruler-straight and she always wore it in a severe bun coiled tightly at her nape. Usually a pencil or two could be found stabbed into the Olive-Oyl-type knot. And her face—without a trace of makeup, which was the norm for her—looked no older than a teenager's. The glasses that rested heavily on the tip of her delicate nose were huge and thick with tortoiseshell rims. They were far too overpowering for her gamine features. She reminded him of one of the geeky, tagalong kid sisters that one of his friends in high school used to gripe about all the time. Yeesh.... Definitely not for him.

But worse by far than her size, or her hair, or even her glasses, was the ugly postal uniform she wore day in and day out. Patches and pockets and blue regulation fabric that would make even the ultrafeminine BambiAnn look like a frump. He didn't think he'd ever seen Wendy wearing anything else.

And those shoes. Good Lord. Those hideous black clodhoppers had to weigh a ton.

Travis knew that Dusty wanted him to fall madly in love with Wendy and make her his mommy. But, dagnabbit anyway, as much as he hated to disappoint the little squirt, when hell finally froze over and he decided to make the idiotic mistake of getting married again, it wouldn't be to "one of the boys," like Wendy.

Deciding it was time to give poor Wendy a much needed break from his active son, Travis hopped out of his truck and bounded across her yard. As he drew nearer, he could hear his son's giddy laughter. He knew that the punch-drunk hilarity that wafted out to greet him signaled that it was way past bedtime for one staggering bundle of energy. Travis smiled to himself at the infectious sound. Dusty was the only good thing that had come out of his debacle of a marriage to Elly Mae. Peering through the darkness, he located the doorbell and alerted Wendy to his arrival.

"Dusty," Wendy pleaded patiently, peeling the small boy from around her waist, "let go."

"You ain't gettin' away that easy, you yellow-bellied cactus head!" Dusty giggled and tightened his grip.

Wendy laughed. "Cactus head?" She picked the boy up and threw his light frame over her shoulder. "Who you callin' a cactus head?" she asked, playfully thumping his bottom.

"You!" he crowed. Bobbing along upside down, he returned the thumps to her bottom as she made her way to the door.

Flipping on the porch light, she peeked through the peephole and then unlocked the dead bolt. Just as she'd suspected, it was Travis. It was about time, she thought disgruntledly. A quick glance at the clock on the hall table told her that it was after midnight. This was his fourth date this week. Whatever she apparently lacked in social skills, he seemed to make up for, in spades. The man had more dates than a Christmas fruitcake. Shaking her head, she pulled open the door and found him standing there, looking for all the world like Brad Pitt after a rough ride with Thelma and Louise. She allowed Dusty to slide to the floor and stood back to make room for Travis.

"Come on in." She motioned, pushing her glasses up on her nose so that she could better sniff the air. "Good heavens," she said, wrinkling her nose in disdain. "You smell like the toilet-water counter at the five-and-dime."

Travis dimpled as he caught his son midair and swung the noisy child up onto his back. "Yeah, BambiAnn gave it her best shot tonight, but I told her I had to get home to you." He winked devilishly.

"Oh, please, spare me the details." Turning, Wendy led them to the living room where she began gathering up Dustin's belongings and stuffing them into his knapsack.

"Dad! Dad!" Dusty shouted, interrupting joyfully. "We built a tent in the living room and I had chocolate milk for dinner."

Travis lifted his cowboy hat off his son's head and slid it easily onto his own thick brown hair. "No kidding? Sounds like you had a good time. Did you tell Wendy thank you?"

"'Course." Dusty rolled his eyes. "'Bout a million times."

Travis looked at Wendy, who nodded in verification. If there was one thing she admired about her wild-man, womanizing, devil-may-care neighbor, it was the way he was raising his son. It was evident that he loved the boy to distraction. It seemed to be the only thing, as far as she could tell, that he actually cared about.

"Good." Travis nodded and set Dusty on his feet. "Give Wendy a hand straightening up, will you? It looks like a bomb went off in here." Scratching his head, Travis stared in wonder at the living room, and then at Wendy. He grinned easily. "Hey, I'm really sorry about doing this to you so often over the past few weeks. I'm working on getting a new, permanent sitter for Dusty, but these things take time."

"I don't mind, really," Wendy said, shrugging lightly. "I love the company." Sinking down onto the couch, she began stuffing napkins and cookie wrappers into the brown bag that had held their peanut butter and jelly rations.

Travis stretched tiredly, then joined her on the couch. With a little prodding, he finally had his son folding the tent blankets and dragging the dining room chairs back to the table.

"Man, am I tired, or—" Travis stared intently at the coffee table in front of him "—what?" he asked distractedly.

Wendy felt her stomach sink. The books. Damn. She should have known better than to leave them out for all the world to see. Before she knew it, the entire population of New Hope, Texas, would know that she was on a quest. A quest to become engaged before she turned thirty. It was humiliating. Travis would undoubtedly tell someone and the word would spread like wildfire. They had a lot of the same friends. People would find out. She sighed.

On the other hand, what difference did it make? It was no secret that she was pretty much of a flop in the ingenue department. She didn't exactly have dates knocking down her door the way Travis did. On a good day, his driveway did more business than a convenience store. She ought to know. Sometimes the overflow blocked her driveway.

Lifting his eyes, he arched a skeptical brow and smirked. *"How To Hook a Husband?"* He chuckled and reached for the stack of books and magazines. "What the hell is this? You're... hunting for a husband?" Hooting at the ceiling, he pushed his hat back and let the laughter flow.

Reaching over, Wendy snatched her precious books from his arms and stuffed them under the pillows that supported her elbow.

"It's not funny, you big Neanderthal," she huffed defensively. Smacking the pillows, she glowered at him through narrowed eyes. "This happens to be research." Wendy had always loved research. Approaching this husband hunt in a scholarly fashion was the only thing that had made it bearable. How dare this...this...playboy—without a single physical flaw—make fun of her? He had no idea what she was going through. It made her blood boil. "*Serious* research," she reiterated, elbowing him grumpily on the arm. She fought the urge to smack his gorgeous, perfect face. "So, I'd appreciate it if you'd stop laughing."

"Why?"

She waited for Dusty to drag another chair toward the dining room before she continued. "Why what?" she snapped.

He snorted. "Why all the advice on how to land a man?"

"Because," she cried, "I'm going to be thirty!" She stared plaintively at him, as though this fact explained everything.

"So?" Travis shrugged, puzzled.

"So." Wendy sighed, exasperated at the obtuse male mind. "The article says that once a woman is past thirty, her chances of finding a mate are slim to none."

"What article?"

"The one I found in a magazine in the recycling bin down at the post office. It said that once you reach the critical age of thirty, there is a shortage of men. If you haven't...uh..."

"Bagged one?" Travis supplied helpfully.

"Yes," she said snippily. "*Bagged* one by then, chances are you'll go to your grave an old spinster."

Travis looked at her as though she'd lost her marbles. "So you're going to be thirty. Big deal. I turned thirty over three years ago and it hasn't affected my love life." He grinned rakishly, deep dimples cutting crescents in his cheeks, and adjusted his cowboy hat on his head.

Darting a disgusted glance at the overhead light fixture, Wendy pointed at him. "Yeah, well, I'm not the alley cat you are. I haven't made a career out of dating people I barely know."

It was true. Wendy had overlooked her social life in favor of making a career out of the postal service. Growing up, she'd always known that she was a plain Jane. That was the way her parents had liked it. They'd encouraged her studious life-style. It was a wonder she'd had the courage to move out from under their overly protective, domineering wings back home in Louisiana, and take the postmistress job in New Hope.

"She's our little bookworm," her father would boast. "Spelling champion five years in a row."

"She's my *good* girl," her mother would sniff. "More important things on her mind than running around with a bunch of boys."

"She's a bore," her younger sister, Wild Wanda—the family black sheep—would taunt. "She'll never get a date."

They were *all* right, Wendy decided, letting her head loll miserably back against the floral pattern of the couch's upholstery. When had she allowed life's normal milestones to pass her by unnoticed? She'd missed out on everything from the prom to dating to marriage to kids, while Wanda had enthusiastically dated every member of the football team, including the second string. When had it become her duty to make up for her parents' disappointment in her free-spirited sister? And, worst of all, how had she let the years slip away, without realizing that once she made it over the hill, there were no men waiting on the other side?

She'd blown it. Being pigeonholed at an early age by her family and being afraid to rock the boat, she had just found it easier to go with the flow. The maddening thing was, it was as much her fault as anyone's.

Well, by golly, not anymore. No more Miss Nice Guy. Things were going to be different from now on. Wouldn't her prim and proper folks be surprised at Thanksgiving when she showed up with a new attitude and a new fiancé? A sense of purpose surged through Wendy, and she tensed like an animal poised for a fight to the death. She would give sister Wanda a run for her money in the shocking department. Yes. She knew she'd have to hustle, with a single-mindedness that she hadn't utilized since dead week before college finals.

Setting her jaw with determination, she glared at Travis. "I'm going to be engaged by my thirtieth birthday," she announced grimly. "Or know the reason why."

His brows rose curiously. "When is your thirtieth birthday?"

"December first."

Travis frowned as he did some quick calculating. "That's only about a month away."

"Yep. The Tuesday after the Russo wedding. With any luck, I'll attend the wedding on my intended's arm." She stole a glance up at him. "That's my goal, at any rate."

The young, happily betrothed were friends of Travis and Wendy. Back in February, they'd both attended an engagement party thrown by their mutual friend, Faith Harper, for Michael Russo and Michelle Parker. Travis had attended with the giggling and jiggling BambiAnn Howe. Wendy had gone stag. She'd never forget the feeling of melancholy that had stayed with her for days after that party. Everyone, it seemed, had at least *some* experience at love. Everyone, except of course, for her.

No more. She was through with the wallflower act. Time to burst out of the cocoon and spread her wings.

"Do you have anyone in mind?" Travis asked, doubt oozing from every syllable.

Again she waited for Dusty to disappear into her dining room with another chair. "I'm going to make a list," she said defensively. Leaning forward, she grew thoughtful. "Hey, you work with a lot of men, maybe you could help."

"Maybe," he said distractedly, staring at the nymphet who pouted prettily at him from the cover of the *Metropolitan* magazine.

Wendy followed his gaze. So. Men went for that type, huh? Well, it was clear she'd have to save up her money and buy herself a bustline if she was ever going to compete with that. No time, she decided, watching Travis in fascination as he went into a hormonally induced trance over the bi-kini-clad model.

She would just have to make the best of the assets she had. Besides, a little tissue here and there and she'd sport a perky little shelf of cleavage that would have Travis looking twice. She shook her head. Who cared what Travis thought? She had to zero in on an available man and figure out what turned him on, then set out to achieve that look. Yep, she thought triumphantly, this couldn't be any harder than the calculus classes she'd taken in college. Heck, if dough-for-brains BambiAnn could figure it out, she could.

Finally, Travis tore his eyes away from the cover girl and read the caption out loud. Angling his head toward her, he asked sardonically, "Do you have what it takes to snare a man?"

"Maybe not now, but I can get it."

Travis cast a doubtful glance down at her work shoes, and his expression grew more dubious as his eyes traveled north. "Okay..." The word came out with a slow hiss of air.

Unable to stand it anymore, Wendy hauled off and punched him in the shoulder. Ow. What was he wearing under that ratty work shirt? Armor? She shook her hand to lessen the pain. "Okay, so I may not be a blond sexpot like BimboAnn..."

"BambiAnn," Travis corrected, grinning good-naturedly.

"*Bambi*Ann," she stressed. "But with some research, I can learn. How hard can it be? If BambiAnn can get it together to snare a man, surely I can."

He shook his head slowly, and it was obvious that he thought she was a lost cause. This only served to fuel Wendy's righteous indignation and sense of purpose.

"Hey," she cried as a light bulb flared to life above her head. "You date a lot of sexpots. Maybe you could give me some pointers." Twisting eagerly on the couch next to him, she leaned forward and tapped him with excitement on the knee. "How about if I make a deal with you. I'll baby-sit Dusty evenings and weekends while you alley cat around, in exchange for lessons on how to be sexier." She beamed at him, inordinately pleased with herself.

Travis blinked, his jaw dropping. "How the hell am I supposed to do that?"

Prickly heat stole into her cheeks. Good heavens. He didn't have to be quite so frank with her. "Well, I don't know, exactly. I've never done anything like this before." Truth be told, she'd only had a handful of very painful and embarrassing dates in her entire life. Of course, this would only confirm his premise that she was a lost cause. "I suppose we could start by you teaching me to make small talk and, uh, dance and, well...pretty much everything. My, uh, experience, when it comes to dating is very limited. I've only been out a few times." The twin spots of heat on the crests of her cheeks grew impossibly hotter.

As Travis sat, watching Wendy squirm, his heart went out to her. Geez. Why was she going to put herself through all this emotional turmoil, only to end up empty-handed? It was a mugs game. But, hey, he thought—listening to Dusty scrape chairs into place at the dining room table and clump around the floor folding blankets—he could sure as heck use the baby-sitter. Maybe he should take her up on the hare-brained scheme. It appeared that it would benefit them both. Although, he had to admit, he was getting the better end of the bargain. Lost cause or no, it was at least worth a try. There had to be some poor guy out there who wouldn't mind having a guy like Wendy as a wife. Ugly shoes and all.

He shrugged. "Sure. It's a deal." Smiling what he hoped was a reassuring smile, he asked, "When do you want to get started?"

Wendy rubbed her heart-shaped chin thoughtfully. "I don't have much time, really. It's only five weeks till the Russo wedding." Five more weeks till she crested the infamous *hill* and began her descent on the other side. The side that was quite literally a no-man's-land. "And, I'll be thirty, three days after that…so, how about if we get started on my lessons on Monday? After work?"

That should give her some time to do a little prep work. Read her books, take the quizzes in the magazines, try some makeover tips. In general, prepare as though she were getting ready for an exam.

Travis thoughtfully chewed his lower lip. "Monday?"

"Or Tuesday," she hedged, embarrassed that she'd taken for granted that he'd be free. Knowing him, he had a date. Several dates. "Whatever you want," she said, waving her hands nonchalantly in the air.

"Monday's fine," Travis agreed, removing his hat and punching what he called a Texas bull-riding-curve into the brim, before popping it back on his head. "Dusty," he called, disentangling his lanky frame from behind her coffee table and standing. He stamped his feet to get the blood running. "You about done in there?"

"Yeah," came the muffled cry. "I'm folding the big blanket."

"Well, get a move on. I want to hit the hay before the sun comes up." Travis arched back, stretching and yawning.

"Okay." Dusty giggled as he stumbled over his feet.

Travis regarded Wendy through the hoods of his sleepy eyes. "Thanks again for looking after the squirt for me. I don't know what I'd have done without you this month."

"No problem," Wendy reassured him, and moved with him to the center of the room, where they gathered Dusty's supplies. "My pleasure. He's such a good kid."

Travis smiled indulgently. "He is, isn't he?"

"The best."

They stood for a moment, smiling at each other, two friends, easy with each other's company after three years of being good neighbors. Travis took Dusty's knapsack from Wendy's arms and led the way to her front hallway.

"Hey, I almost forgot. I got the bid on the post office remodel. I'm squeezing it in before a couple of big jobs I have lined up, so I'm going to be starting on Monday. Hope that's okay."

Wendy fairly beamed at him. "Oh, hallelujah!" She clapped her hands in delight, bringing the dimples out again in his cheeks.

He turned to face her, his hand resting on the front doorknob. With a twist, he pulled it open and the crickets' song filtered in from the shadows beyond.

"There will probably be quite a bit of dust and racket for a while." He lifted and dropped his shoulders. "Can't be helped."

"Oh, I don't care. Make all the noise you want. I've been looking forward to this for ages."

"I know." Boy, oh, boy, he knew. "We could probably carpool on Monday. That is, if you want. No sense in driving two vehicles all that way, when we just live a stone's throw from each other."

"Okay. Shall you drive, or shall I?"

"Me. I've got all my tools and stuff in the box on my truck."

"Sure. Okay. Great. Golly. More square footage. I can hardly wait. That dinky back room has been driving me crazy for three years. This town is too big for such a small post office."

Travis nodded in agreement. "Dusty," he called again, exasperated. "Step on it." He rolled his eyes at Wendy. "He's a dawdler."

"Unless chocolate milk is involved." She smiled fondly in the direction of her dining room.

"I guess we could get started on your lessons after work, if you want. Any ideas where we should meet?"

"I don't care. We could meet here."

Travis frowned. "Nah, why don't you come over to my place instead. That way Dusty can play in his room and stay out from under our feet. I can put him to bed at a decent hour for once." He sent her a sheepish look. "Speaking of going to bed, I'd better go find out what's keeping him."

Together, Wendy and Travis made their way to her dining room, only to find young Dustin Donovan fast asleep in the middle of the blanket he'd been folding. His father's cowboy boots were barely on his feet, askew at crazy right angles, and his face, cherubic in repose, was nearly divine in its perfection. They stood, the two adults, sharing the sweet moment and smiling at each other in easy camaraderie.

For if there was one thing they had in common, it was their love for Dusty.

2

After an invigorating shower the next morning, Wendy stood at the entrance to her walk-in closet and stared morosely at her limited clothing options. On the left side of the closet, hanging in a row, were her neatly pressed postal uniforms. Beneath them—freshly polished and shined—lay two pairs of regulation black postal shoes. The heavy-duty type.

The back of the closet was completely empty, except for her black wool winter coat, which came out very infrequently as snowstorms in Texas were rare. On the right side of the closet hung her Sunday dresses. Four dowdy, drably colored dresses, one for each Sunday of the month. One pair of open-toed shoes with low, wide and very sensible heels sat on the floor, waiting for Sunday to arrive. Next to the dresses were two polyester pantsuits, white for summer and postal blue for winter. These she wore on her time off.

Wincing, she snatched the polyester suits off their hangers and stuffed them into the charity bag. What on earth had possessed her to buy these things, let alone wear them? They looked like something straight out of her mother's closet. And even her mother was far too young to wear this style in public.

Well, she thought with determination, Mother wasn't here to dictate her wardrobe today. The Sunday dresses followed the pantsuits into the bag, along with her ridiculously durable and clunky dress pumps. She felt a swift surge of exhilarating liberation from her past. It was no small wonder that no man had ever given her a second look. None of the models in the magazines she'd bought yesterday wore this stuff. She doubted that the models for a senior citizens' magazine would be caught dead in her clothes. Whisking her summer shawl off the top shelf, she threw it into the bag with the rest.

It was clear she was going to have to hit the mall, and hit it hard. And, she would need advice. All the advice she could get on everything she'd flunked in the *Metropolitan* magazine quiz. Clothing, hair, makeup. . . .

Hmm, she mused as she tossed her rejects to the middle of the bedroom floor. Travis would help her with the social skills, but she didn't think he'd be much help on a shopping spree at the mall or on a visit to the beauty shop.

Sagging down onto the edge of her bed, she racked her brain. No one in New Hope wore more makeup than Sue Ellen down at the New Hope diner. For that matter, the forty-five-year-old, thrice-divorced Sue Ellen also had the biggest hair. Maybe she should start the day with breakfast down at the diner, and pick Sue Ellen's brain about the use of cosmetics. Maybe Sue Ellen would have some tips on the clothing front, as well. After all, Sue Ellen must be somewhat of an expert on how to hook a husband. She'd managed to bag three so far.

That decided, Wendy dusted her hands and looked around for something to wear. She made a mental note to add casual clothes to her shopping list. But for now, she'd just have to make due with a postal uniform.

After hurriedly dressing, she twisted her hair into its standard tight bun at the back of her neck. She would experiment with new hairstyles tonight. And, she decided as she adjusted her glasses, maybe a visit to one of those optical shops at the mall was in order. She could get some of those exotic-colored contact lenses. A shiver of excitement traveled up her arms, leaving a wake of gooseflesh as it went. This was fun.

She'd been out from under her parents' strict rule for more than three years now. Why had she waited so long to start living? Where had the time gone? Just yesterday, it seemed, she was graduating from high school. Well, every second that ticked by on the clock was another second lost.

Today was the first day of the rest of her life, and all that nonsense. Time to get down to the business of living, she thought giddily, and rushed headlong to her living room to gather her small clutch purse and car keys.

"And Wendy said when she was little like me she wore a really neat Indian costume and won first prize. She said it was made out of a burpy bag."

"Burlap bag?" Travis stopped waxing the hood of his truck for a moment and shot a sidelong glance at Dustin, who hovered in their driveway at his elbow, extolling—yet again—Wendy Wilcox's virtues. Sometimes he thought if he heard Wendy's name just one more time he'd lose his mind. The kid had a one-track mind. The Wendy track.

"Yeah, Wendy said she would make me one just like it someday with feathers and arrows and everything. I could go Tricken Treaten in *that!*" he shouted up at his father, delighted with the fantasy that played in his mind. Moving along as his father polished his truck, Dustin scratched his nose with the palm of his hand. "Only this year I want to be Casper. Wendy said Casper would be easy to make. It's only eight more days till Halloween and Wendy said..." Dusty spied Wendy coming out onto her front porch. "There she *is,* Dad!" Spinning on his heel, the child stumbled, feet after knees, across the driveway and straight into Wendy's arms. "*Wendy!*"

"Hiya, Sport-o!" Wendy ruffled Dusty's hair affectionately and allowed him to tug her over to where his father stood buffing the hood of his truck. Travis's shirt was unbuttoned and the tails flapped around his jeans-clad thighs with his efforts. No wonder he did so much business in the dating department, she thought absently. He was like something out of a diet soda commercial. The only thing missing was his usual drooling fan club. For a moment she stood, appreciating the way his muscles rippled and his skin glistened with a sheen of perspiration in the fall sunshine. She appreciated the view the way an art connoisseur would appreciate a painting. With objectivity.

She knew that he would never in a million years ever take an interest in her. In a way, that's what Wendy liked about Travis. Because of this fact, she was able to relax around him and just be herself. It didn't bother her that he didn't find her attractive. He wasn't exactly what she was looking for in husband material, either. No. Wendy wanted someone who was ready to settle down. To commit. To put away the wild life and enjoy family life.

"Dad, can I ask her?"

Travis stopped polishing his truck and straightened. "Aw, Dusty, give poor Wendy a break, will ya?" He mopped his brow on his shirtsleeve and sent a beleaguered look at his son.

"What?" Wendy asked, glancing back and forth between father and son.

Dustin barreled ahead. "I want to know if we can make a Casper costume on your sewing machine pretty soon. It's Tricken Treaten in eight more days."

"Sure," Wendy said, and smiled at Travis.

Travis shook his head and shifted the toothpick that he was chewing to the other corner of his mouth. "You don't have to do that. We've imposed on you enough lately. I could just buy him a costume down at the five-and-dime."

Dusty's lip began to tremble. "But, Dad, I don't want a store-bought costume like all the other kids. I want Wendy to make me a Casper costume. Wendy said we can make a

really neat-o one on her sewing machine. Right, Wendy?"
He trained his large, liquid blue eyes up at her.

It was at times like this when Travis was especially hurt by
his ex-wife's defection. How she could just up and leave a
great kid like Dusty was beyond him. But luckily he'd managed to work through the bitterness he felt toward Elly Mae,
and was left with only pity for her. She didn't know what she
was missing.

Travis put his hands on his hips and watched as Wendy
pulled his son up against the stiff fabric of her postal uniform and smoothed his longish golden hair out of his eyes.
How Dusty craved a woman's touch. He knew that his son
didn't care about the Casper costume as much as he wanted
someone to think he was special enough to fuss over. Thank
God, Wendy did. He was starting to think that maybe Dusty
was on to something when it came to their stodgy neighbor.
She was pretty special, really.

"I think making a Casper costume sounds like almost as
much fun as building a tent in the living room. Listen,"
Wendy said, checking her watch, "I have some things I have
to do in town today, so why don't you have your dad bring
you over later this afternoon and we can get started. I have
some old sheets that will work perfectly and you can bring
your Casper lunch box and we'll do our best to copy it,
okay?"

"Okay!" Dustin shrieked and ran around in frenzied circles.

Travis looked over his son's head at Wendy and smiled a
gentle smile of thanks. Wendy stood for a moment, smiling
back, basking in his approval, then with a silent nod of
goodbye for the father, and a quick kiss on the cheek for the
son, she hopped into her car and was gone.

"Hey, Beth, what are you doing here?" Wendy asked the
cute blond teen as she settled onto a stool at the counter at

the diner. "I thought you already had a job, working for Faith over at the Baby Boutique."

Beth grinned and poured Wendy a piping hot cup of coffee. "I do. I'm just giving Sue Ellen a hand for the Saturday breakfast shift. Ever since Kathy went off to college, she's been a little shorthanded."

"Mmm." Wendy nodded and took a sip of her coffee. "Travis is noticing her absence, too. He's still looking for a nanny for Dusty." She glanced around the funky interior of the diner. The smell of sizzling bacon permeated the room and the low murmur of conversation and clanking silverware underscored her question. "Is Sue Ellen here?"

Beth nodded and tucked her pencil in behind her ear. "She stepped into the back room for a minute. She should be back any second. You want to order breakfast? There's still time."

Wendy decided on a short stack of pancakes, and as Beth returned with her order, Sue Ellen emerged from the back. Spotting Wendy, she smiled broadly.

"Hi, Wendy! What brings you to town on a Saturday morning?" She wandered up beside Beth and, leaning across the counter, moved the syrup bottle out of Wendy's way. The diner was clearing out, so she and Beth settled in to shoot the breeze with the local postmistress.

Swallowing her bite of pancake, Wendy set her fork on her plate and dabbed at her mouth with her napkin. "Well, actually, I had a favor to ask you," she said, and peeped up at Sue Ellen over the heavy rim of her glasses. Then she shot a shy glance over at the trendily togged teen. It was obvious that this kid had her finger on the New Hope fashion pulse. "You, too, Beth."

Sue Ellen and Beth exchanged curious glances. "Shoot, honey," Sue Ellen demanded, patting her hugely teased bouffant hairdo with her long, blindingly bright press-on nails.

Wendy licked her lips and cleared her throat. She felt like an idiot. Here she was, nearly over the hill, for crying out loud, asking for help picking out clothes and makeup. It was worth it if she ended up with a husband and a baby, she decided. Setting her chin with determination, she forged doggedly ahead. "Well, the other day I read this article—" She fished the offending article out of her purse and tossed it on the countertop in front of Sue Ellen. "I found the magazine in the recycling bin over at the post office."

Beth and Sue Ellen scanned the article. "What's the problem?" Beth asked, not making the connection.

"I'm going to be thirty on December first." Wendy looked balefully up at them.

"Ohhhh..." they breathed, and looked sympathetically at her.

"I know I need to make some changes in my, uh, look," she admitted, casting her eyes uneasily at her hands. She blinked up at them. "I flunked the *Metropolitan* magazine quiz this month."

"The Do You Have What It Takes To Snare A Man quiz?" Sue Ellen asked.

Wendy nodded.

"Ohhhh..." they breathed again, and exchanged knowing glances.

"My goal is to be engaged by the Russo wedding." Noting the surprise in their expressions, she cringed. Suddenly the plan seemed so ludicrous.

"Isn't the Russo wedding Thanksgiving weekend?" Sue Ellen frowned. "Honey, that's only a little more'n a month away."

"I know. It's the weekend before I turn thirty." Wendy looked desolately at them. "Forget it. It'll never work. It was a dumb idea."

Sue Ellen reached out and grasped her hands. "Don't say that, honey. I love a challenge." She glanced at the calendar on the wall. "I've often thought that with a few modifications you would be a real beauty. You have all the basics. We just need to...enhance them,'' she said, reaching across the counter and tilting Wendy's chin up toward the light.

Wendy's brow puckered. A real beauty? Was Sue Ellen talking about her? She glanced around to see if someone was standing behind her. Someone with the potential to be beautiful.

''We have plenty of time to whip you into shape and snare you a man.'' Laughing, she gave Wendy's arm a quick pat and batted her false eyelashes teasingly. ''I should know, I've done it often enough. But...'' She suddenly frowned. ''We should probably get started right away...hmm. Second shift will be here in half an hour. How about if I go home and get my supplies from my beauty school days. And Beth—'' Sue Ellen turned toward the teen ''—why don't you take Wendy to the mall for a while, and I'll meet you both at her place at say...'' She checked her watch. ''One-thirty?''

''Perf.'' Beth nodded, untying her apron and tossing it onto the counter. Looking expectantly at Wendy, she announced, ''We'd better beat cheek if we're gonna catch all my fave sale racks.''

''Uh...'' Wendy scrambled off her stool and, tossing some bills on the table, hurried after Beth. ''Okay, sure.''

''I'm kind of rusty on this color thing, so you'll have to bear with me,'' Sue Ellen explained, mixing Wendy's hair color like a mad chemist at the kitchen sink. ''I never did like doing color. Always scared the hell out of me.'' She held the bottle of Sunblond Goddess No. 8 up and squinted thoughtfully. ''Do you want to be a goddess or honey-streaked?'' She pursed her lips and poured a little of each tint into the container. ''You'll be a honey-streaked, sun-blond goddess.''

Beth giggled.

"You're not making me feel very confident," Wendy moaned, barely daring to move her mud-caked lips. Sue Ellen was giving her the works. She glanced over at Beth, who sat at her kitchen table hunched over her sewing machine doing heaven only knew what to one of her postal uniforms.

The teen had dragged her at top speed through the mall, shoving the most outlandish outfits into her arms. Wendy grimaced at the thought of her next credit-card bill. "Sue Ellen?" she squeaked, holding her mouth very still.

"Hmm?" The older woman sounded slightly befuddled.

"How come you never worked at a beauty shop?" This little tidbit concerned Wendy.

"I flunked out of beauty school."

"Why?" Wendy asked tentatively.

"I accidentally used hundred-thirty-volume peroxide on a lady's head. Melted her damn hair off." She laughed boisterously. "You should have seen her run screaming out of the beauty school salon. I wasn't far behind her. Turned in my teasing comb, as they say."

"Oh." Wendy didn't want to look a gift horse in the mouth, but really, mousy brown hair was better than none. Quite frankly she didn't think she'd be happy with a man who was attracted to the Kojak look. "So, Beth," she queried, more to take her mind off her hair than any real curiosity, "how's Faith doing these days?" Eight months pregnant, Faith Harper was the owner of New Hope's Baby Boutique where Beth worked part-time.

Beth stopped sewing for a moment and grinned. "Huge. Says she can't wait to have Amelia Rose."

"Amelia Rose, huh? She knows it's going to be a girl?" Wendy asked, wincing as Sue Ellen—in preparation for tinting—raked a snarl out of her hair.

"No." Beth shook her head and shrugged. "Just a gut feeling, I guess."

Wendy's brow furrowed slightly. "But what if it's a boy?"

Sue Ellen stopped ripping the tangles out of Wendy's hair long enough to snort. "Well, with a name like Amelia Rose, he'll have to be a tough little bugger."

"She's going to be a great mom," Wendy said wistfully, wishing for the day when she would bring her own baby into the world. A little child to call her own. A little child like Dusty.

"Yeah," Beth agreed. "She still won't tell anyone who the father is," she mumbled around a mouthful of pins.

Wendy wondered grumpily if the poor thing had been anywhere near her wild-man neighbor eight months ago. No, that wasn't fair, she thought. Travis might have an overactive social life, but he wasn't a cad.

Faith's pregnancy was the most intriguing mystery to hit New Hope in years. Wendy knew that the identity of the unmarried Faith's lover had more than one tongue wagging down at the post office. And, even though Faith was nearly as straitlaced as Wendy, there didn't seem to be any wedding in sight. The whole thing was so unlike Faith. Wendy guessed that's what made it so interesting to everyone. It sure gave the New Hope Senior Citizen Stamp Collecting Club—also known as the N.H.S.C.S.C.C.—something to flap their jaws and clutch their bosoms about.

The sounds of feet stamping on her back porch drew Wendy from her ruminations.

"Hello," Travis called, letting himself and his son into her kitchen through the back door. "Figured you'd probably be back by now—" His eyes widened imperceptibly as he moved toward Wendy.

"Wow, Wendy." Dustin raced over to her chair and stared at her facial mask and perm rods in awe. "Is that what you're wearin' for Tricken Treaten?"

Travis coughed and clapped his hand over his son's mouth. "Son," he explained, unsuccessfully attempting to swallow the mirth that swelled into his throat, "this is what ladies do to make themselves look beautiful." Unable to hold back, Travis guffawed rudely at the ceiling.

"But I think Wendy's beautiful just the way she is," Dustin staunchly defended the love of his life.

"Well, in a way you're right," Travis drawled, and winked broadly at his seething neighbor. "I guess you'll understand when you're older."

"You always say that," the boy complained.

Travis covered his grin with his free hand. "That's because it's true."

Sue Ellen nudged them out of the way. "Hey, Travis. Dusty. Why don't you guys beat it? I'm trying to mix these chemicals and I don't want to screw it up."

"But Wendy is going to sew my Casper costume now," Dusty explained up at the beauty school dropout.

"Sweetheart." Wendy held her hand out to the worried boy. "This is taking just a little longer than expected." Travis snorted and Wendy shot him a quelling glare. "So why don't you come back in a couple hours and we'll get you all fixed up. You and your dad could come over for dinner."

"Promise?" he asked, shades of his mother's desertion creeping into his small voice.

"Cross my heart, hope to die." She nodded solemnly. She held out her pinkie and hooked it with his. "Give me a kiss."

Ignoring the cracked green facial mask, Dustin puckered up and planted a noisy smack on her cheek.

And something melted in the vicinity of Travis's heart.

He cleared his throat. "We'll go pick up some takeout for dinner since you probably won't get around to cooking," he told her, glancing dubiously around the biology lab that was her kitchen. "Tacos okay?"

Dusty jumped up and down for joy.

"Fine." Because of the stiff green gunk she wore on her face, she didn't dare smile with her lips, but her eyes spoke to him of her gratitude.

Wendy stood in front of her full-length mirror and stared in amazement at her made-over reflection. "Oh..." was all she was able to utter. Moving her eyes slightly, she caught the satisfied looks of approval that Beth and Sue Ellen were exchanging behind her back. She hated to disappoint them, especially after all their hard work, but she'd never felt more foolish in her entire life. "I don't know..." she began doubtfully. "It's so..."

"Radical," Beth supplied.

"Alluring," Sue Ellen put in helpfully.

Wendy guessed that was one way to look at it. Gone was the straight brown length of rope that had hung for years down her back or rested in a coil on her neck. Now her shoulder-length hair stood out at right angles in layers of wild, curly, honey-streaked, sun-blond-goddess corkscrews. Sue Ellen had used at least half a bottle of hair spray and styling gel to get them to stand straight out at attention that way. For one hysterical moment, Wendy wondered if Sue Ellen had raided Phyllis Diller's fright wig collection. Good Lord, she was going to have to cut special notches in her door frames just to get from room to room. It was a good thing Travis was remodeling the post office. Perhaps she could request extra-wide doorways.

No wonder she'd never gone in for the fashion scene. It had taken her the whole dang day just to get dressed. She blinked rapidly. Apparently false eyelashes and contact lenses did not mix. The aquamarine lenses that she'd picked up at the mall's Hour Optical that morning stared eerily back at her in an otherworldly, almost extraterrestrial kind of way. They matched the streaks of bright blue eye shadow that Sue Ellen had assured her would have the men dropping like flies. False eyelashes like giant desert spiders dangled from her eyelids, and Wendy tentatively batted her eyes in what she hoped was a coquettish maneuver.

Was all this too much? she wondered, struck by the sudden impression that anyone with eyes this black and blue should be on their way to the hospital. None of the models on the cover of *Metropolitan* seemed to wear quite this much makeup.

Nor this little clothing.

Her gaze traveled lower to the renovation job Beth had done on her postal uniform. What had originally been a regulation shirt and trousers was now nothing more than an indecent pair of hot pants and a scrappy little halter top with the sleeves' postal patches moved to the front. Even though Beth had left the regulation belt and tie, this getup would never pass muster with the higher-ups. Would it? She knew of women who worked for the postal service that opted not to wear the uniform, or took a fashionable nip and tuck in the unflattering shirt and pants, but *this?* She glanced over at Beth, who was glowing with approval.

"That special bra we bought you really makes the most of your curves. Nobody could miss them now," Beth claimed enthusiastically. The girl waved her hand toward Wendy's cleavage as it peeped fetchingly through the peek a boo hole she'd fashioned across the front of the daringly cropped top.

"Oh, yes," Sue Ellen agreed. "And with your shapely little legs, those hot pants and the new four-inch platforms are perfect."

Wendy chewed the inside of her cheek. She guessed—for the time being anyway—it would have to do. In the carefree style of Edward Scissorhands, Beth had joyfully attacked all five of her uniforms. This being the weekend, there was no way she could chicken out and slip back into the Frowzy Zone.

Tugging on the hot pants, she could remember the woman across the street wearing them when she was a kid. Her mother had kicked up a fuss when she noticed Wendy's father covertly watching "that brazen hussy" through the blinds. Wendy grinned at the memory. She'd missed out on making this particular fashion statement the first time around. Did she want to hop on the bandwagon this time? She squinted, trying to get the whole picture, the way Sue Ellen and Beth saw it. Unfortunately, all she could see staring back at her was BambiAnn's twin sister.

But, she thought, shrugging lightly, as much as she might detest the look, it seemed to work. BambiAnn was never at a loss for men.

All was fair in love and war, as they said. Maybe she should give this new look a try and see where it got her. Time was running out. She had to get radical if she was going to achieve her goal.

"You guys really think we're on the right track with all this...paraphernalia?" she asked, glancing at her friends for reassurance.

"Honey, you're going to set this town on its ear," Sue Ellen told her confidently.

"Go get 'em, Killer." Beth snapped a get-down-mama Z in the air.

Taking a deep, fortifying breath, Wendy nodded, her corkscrew curls bobbing wildly around her head. "Watch out, New Hope, Texas," she cried. "Wendy Wilcox is coming to town. And she is gonna kick some butt and take some names." Smiling broadly, Wendy spun dangerously on her new four-inch heels and enthusiastically high-fived her pals.

"Hi, Wendy! We got tacos!" Dustin crowed, and charged past his father into her house later that day. "And I brought my Casper lunch pail for us to copy tonight."

Travis reached out and touched the shower cap that covered Wendy's hair. "Love that look," he said, his voice dripping with teasing sarcasm.

Wendy slapped his hand away and took the heavily loaded bag fresh from El Taco Taco out from under his arm. "I set the dining room table," she informed him and Dusty as she led the way. "We'll eat in there."

Ambling after her, Travis grinned at her ratty white chenille robe. Looked like she was wearing a damn bedspread. And what was with the white goop she had plastered all over her face now? It was almost worse than the cracked green stuff.

Fortunately, the uninhibited Dustin phrased the question that Travis was reticent to ask. "How come you have white junk on your face now?" He hopped up onto the chair between the two adults and set his legs swinging back and forth as he stared up at her with interest.

Wendy's hand flew to her face. She'd forgotten she was still wearing Phase II. Hopefully it covered the crimson that surely stained her cheeks. "It's a cleansing mask, sweetheart. It's supposed to, uh, 'clean away all the impurities and leave my skin fresh and younger looking,' I think. And the shower cap is to hold the conditioner on my hair to make it 'softer and more luxurious.' Sue Ellen used to sell Mabel Lee beauty products, till she got fired. She left me a bunch of makeup and hair samples."

Loading his plate with Mexican takeout, Travis made one of those masculine sounds deep in his throat that signaled his skepticism. Dropping his paper plate in front of him, he leaned forward on his elbows and scrutinized her face. "I don't know. To me you look worse than before you started with all this nonsense." His good-natured grin took the sting out of his words. "I can see why Sue Ellen got fired."

"Well," Wendy admitted, "she did mention something about causing an almost fatal allergic reaction in one of her clients." She sighed and helped Dusty unwrap his dinner. "And she was so close to earning her golden tiara. With real rhinestones."

"Imagine that," Travis deadpanned.

"You just wait, bucko," Wendy snapped and, grabbing a fistful of paper napkins out of the bag, mopped the cleansing mask off her face. "I'm a work in progress. Come Monday, you won't even recognize me."

"Whatever." Travis grinned around a mouthful of taco.

3

Wendy could tell, as she pulled her door open on Monday morning, that if she'd had a feather in her hand, she could have knocked Travis over with it. As he stood there on her front stoop, gaping at her, his bugging eyes seemed unable to rove fast enough to keep up with the myriad impressions that flitted through his mind. Wendy couldn't be sure if the glazed look on his face was approval or shock.

Deciding to go with approval, she patted her giant, well varnished, honey-streaked, sun-blond-goddess hairdo and strove to look much more confident than she felt. "Ready?" she asked breezily, and clutched at the doorknob in an effort to keep from falling off her new shoes.

His eyes locked on the peek a boo hole that Beth had cut over her bustline. "Oh, yeah," he breathed.

"Okay, hang on just a sec while I go get my purse," she said. Smiling bravely, she let go of the doorknob and tottered unsteadily toward her living room.

Travis swallowed the great wad of shock that had gathered in his throat and licked his dry lips. He wasn't sure which was worse. The new Wendy or the old one. She looked so uncomfortable in her new, outrageous, bimbo garb. Awkward. Gangly. Like a kid who'd gotten into Mommy's closet to play dress-up. He fought the urge to go into the house after her and tell her to wash her face and get dressed. But he knew that would only hurt her feelings, and she was trying so hard. He had to give her credit for that. What she was doing took a lot of guts.

He wondered why some women seemed to be able to pull off the look. BambiAnn, for example. Bright blue eye shadow and hair that an emu could nest in looked natural on her. On Wendy, though, it just looked weird. He liked her better with those ugly glasses and sensible shoes. Sagging against Wendy's door frame, he rubbed the back of his neck. What the hell was he thinking? He'd obviously been listening to his son's adoring prattle for far too long.

However, he had to admit he found himself surprised that she had such a nice figure. A lot more breast than he'd originally given her credit for. Not exactly overly voluptuous, the way he liked 'em, but nice. Slim. Petite. Kind of cute, in a girlish kind of way.

If she would tone down the blond dirigible that had landed on her head, and kill the centipedes she'd glued to her eyes, she'd probably look pretty good.

Something more modest in the uniform department might be in order, as well. Not that he was complaining about finally getting a glimpse of the curves she'd managed to effectively hide all those years. He plunged a shaky hand through his hair. But hell, a getup like that was meant for the bedroom. Not the New Hope post office. Giving his head a little shake to clear the image of Wendy out of the bedroom in his mind, he wondered how he should tell her.

Oh, hell. It was none of his business. He'd stay out of it. She was a bright girl. Let her figure it out for herself.

Lurching toward him on wobbly legs, Wendy slowly made her way back through her foyer, held up her new, king-size purse and smiled bravely. "All set," she chirped, and suddenly, without any warning, pitched headlong down the stairs.

Travis leapt forward, caught her just before she hit the ground and, standing her upright again, balanced her on the stilts she called shoes. Astonishingly enough, her larger-than-life purse had flown, of its own volition, halfway across the yard. Knitting her brows together in consternation, she clutched great handfuls of his shirt to keep from going under once more.

"I, uh..." she stammered, clinging to his buttons and struggling for balance. "It's gonna take a while to, uh, get used to these new shoes..." Her knees buckled and she slid halfway down his body before he was able to help her find her footing again. "Sorry," she squeaked, scaling his chest the way a mountain climber would ascend a sheer cliff.

"It's okay. Um, are you gonna be all right in those... shoes?" he asked, wrapping his arm around her slender waist and pulling her up against his chest. Good grief. He wasn't going to get anything done on the post office if he had to walk around all day with her wrapped around his tool belt. Not that he'd mind, really, he thought, grinning down at her as she valiantly tried to extract her heels from the depths of the front lawn. She had pretty damn good legs. And she was so petite. Delicate. Something about that brought out the protectiveness in him.

"I, uh, seem to be stuck in the—" Wendy looked up at him with a pained expression "—lawn."

"Oh, for pity's sake. Come here," he said, reaching down and scooping her up into his arms.

"Ooo," Wendy squeaked. "You don't have to—"

"Listen," he interrupted as he leaned back, trying to avoid losing an eye to one of her pointy, corkscrew curls. "We can't stand around all day while you learn to walk. I have to get Dustin to school."

"Oh, of course," she breathed, and tightened her hands around his neck.

Moving across her lawn, he snagged the handle of her purse with his work boot and, lifting it up to his hand, looped it over his shoulder. With horrendous effort, Travis kept his eyes out of the peek a boo hole that rode at eye level as he made his way over to his pickup.

It was a good thing he had a king cab. They'd need the extra space for her hair. And for her new purse. He'd never noticed her carrying such a large purse before. It reminded him of the suitcase BambiAnn lugged around. Filled to the brim with cosmetics and other tiresome goop that she was always spritzing and rubbing onto herself.

Women, Travis grunted to himself as he set Wendy on her feet in his driveway next to the passenger door. Dustin was already strapped into the back seat, his Casper lunch pail resting on his knees.

Somehow, with Travis's able assistance, they finally managed to deposit her, sun-blond-goddess corkscrews and all, into the front seat of the impossibly high four-wheel-drive cab. On the count of three, he'd gripped her waist, then, setting her on the running board, supported her thighs as she'd ducked her head and slid into the cab. Travis figured she probably could have made it all right without the thigh support, but he couldn't seem to resist the urge to feel for himself if her upper legs were really as firm as they looked.

"Wow, Wendy!" Dustin chortled from the seat behind her, batting playfully at her hair. "Is *that* what you are going to wear for Tricken Treaten in six more days?"

"That's enough, Dustin," his father admonished as he took his seat behind the wheel and started the engine. Snatching his sunglasses off the visor, he put them on to mask the laughter in his eyes. His sigh was audible.

It was going to be a long damn day.

"What in thunder is wrong with your eye?" Travis looked over the edge of his sunglasses at her as they traveled down the freeway toward New Hope's city center. They'd dropped Dustin off at the Tex Baker grade school, and were now on their way to the post office.

"I don't know." Wendy frowned and blinked crazily. "It feels like I have a chicken in my eye."

"Looks like it, too," Travis muttered.

"Pardon?" Wendy asked as she peered into the small visor mirror.

"Nothing," he said, shrugging amicably.

Wendy still wasn't sure what he was thinking about the changes in her look. Why, he hadn't even mentioned her new hair and uniform.

Men, she thought huffily as she tried to figure out what was irritating her aquamarine contact lens. What good did it do to get up at four in the morning to get all gussied up, when she could have slept three more hours and gotten the same reaction?

That wasn't exactly true, she amended to herself as she dug her eye drops out of her purse. If she'd been wearing her regulation postal shoes, Travis would never have had to carry her to the truck. And, as much as she hated to admit it, the experience had been exhilarating. She'd never been quite that close to such a . . . virile man before. He smelled so good. Something hot and fluttery knotted low in her stomach. She forced herself to concentrate on her eye problem.

"Got it," she said triumphantly, dabbing at her cumbersome lashes with a tissue. "It's a good thing you're driving. I think there should be a warning label on mascara— Don't Wear This Stuff And Drive."

Travis chuckled. "So," he said, glancing in his side mirror before changing into the lane that led to their exit, "you get anywhere on the list of potential husbands yet?"

"Mmm-hmm." Wendy nodded and, rummaging around in her new purse, came up with a pad and pencil. "So far I've only been able to come up with a few eligible bachelors, so, if you can think of anybody, I'll add 'em to my list when we get together after work tonight for our first lesson."

Nodding noncommittally, Travis glanced at her pad. "Who have you got?"

"First of all, there's Cecil Yates."

Travis snorted. "Cecil Yates? That sniveling wimp? Come on, Wendy, you can do better than that. There's a reason he's not married. He's a dork."

"He is not," Wendy retorted hotly. "I'll have you know he's one of the wealthiest men in the state. He's very highly respected in the computer industry."

"He's a weasel," Travis steadfastly maintained. "Stuck-up little prig. Cross him off your list," he instructed.

"I will not!" Wendy scooted closer to her door. "In fact, I think I'll start with him. He always kind of flirts with me when he comes into the post office. I just have to screw up my courage and ask him for a date."

Travis snorted again. "Who else?"

"Conway Brubaker."

"Cross him off, too," Travis demanded in a tightly controlled voice.

"Why?" Wendy cried in exasperation.

"Because he is a womanizing wild man. He'll break your heart."

Wendy's laughter was sharp. "Oh, that's rich. Look who's calling the kettle black. Listen up, Travis, I think Conway Brubaker is one of the nicest men in this part of Texas. He comes from a wonderful, large, loving family. I already think the world of his folks. What could be better than that?"

"Doesn't hurt that he's loaded, too," Travis muttered, glancing over his shoulder as he exited the freeway.

"What are you trying to say?" Wendy demanded, narrowing her twin aquamarine color spots at him.

"Nothing." Travis donned a mask of innocence.

"Good. Because I resent the insinuation that I'm some kind of fortune-hunting gold digger." She waggled a disgruntled finger at him. "Rich people need love, too. Besides, I don't care if he's poor as a church mouse, if he'll make a decent husband someday. If you're so smart, Mr. Donovan, why don't you make a suggestion?''

Travis grinned at her snippy attitude. She was kind of cute when she was all fired up. ''I'll give it some thought, and get back to you with my ideas.''

''Fine.'' Wendy huffed and, taking a deep breath, tried to quell the stage fright that suddenly roared through her gut when she thought about facing the general public with her new look. In a way, she was glad Travis would be there with her. She could use the moral support.

Travis laid down his tape measure and stood listening to the commotion through the wall where the post office boxes were located. The great Elvis-fat-or-skinny-commemorative-stamp debate died abruptly as Agnes, Minny and Ethel caught a glimpse of their postmistress as she stepped behind the counter. The three elderly ladies were members of the New Hope Senior Citizen Stamp Collecting Club and, in general, the town busybodies.

''Good Lord,'' Agnes gasped, clutching her bosom in horror. ''Who is that *tramp?*''

Her throbbing sotto voce comment reached Travis from behind a pearl-buttoned gloved hand. He was reasonably sure that Wendy had caught the remark, as well. Agnes was the president of the N.H.S.C.S.C.C., and led the daily gossip fest at the post office. Travis ought to know. He'd been the subject of many of their scathing discussions. For his part, he didn't give a rat's hind end what Agnes and the gals had to say about him, but it rankled that they could tear down the precious self-esteem that Wendy was working so hard to build.

''I don't know,'' Minny said, fanning herself with her mail. ''If I didn't know better I'd think it was our darling little Wendy.''

''Oh, my wordy,'' Agnes moaned. ''First our darling little Faith gets herself in a family way outside the marriage bed, and now our darling little Wendy is rushing—hot on her heels—down the path of destruction."

"What is the world coming to?" Ethel wondered. Extracting a small flask from her brassiere, she took a quick swig. "Thank heavens I made another soothing batch of the curative." No one in New Hope was exactly sure what went into the curative, but its healing results were immediate if Ethel's flushed cheeks and slightly slurred speech were any indication.

Travis had to restrain himself from bounding out to the front and giving the snooty old birds the bum's rush. How dare they stand there and judge Wendy? Okay, so maybe she'd laid the Mabel Lee makeup samples on a little thick. That wasn't her fault. She was learning, for crying out loud. Give her some time. She'd get the hang of it.

He hated the idea that anyone might take the wind out of her sails. On Dusty's behalf, he felt somewhat protective of the woman that had come to mean so much to his son. And, if he were honest with himself, she'd been a pretty good pal to him, too. He genuinely liked her. It was rare for Travis to actually like a woman. Feel that he could talk to her. Trust her. Ever since the number that Elly Mae had done on him and his son, he'd treated women like playthings. That's what they wanted, wasn't it? Most of the women he knew, that is, except for Wendy. Wendy was different. He would hate like hell to see anything hurt her.

Eventually the three horror-struck stamp collectors were on their way and—as the morning wore on—Travis immersed himself in his work, tearing out walls and clearing debris until the brouhaha out front once again caught his attention.

What the hell? he wondered as he poked his head out of the back room to where Wendy stood behind the front desk. The lobby was literally jammed with men, all ages, shapes and sizes, smiling and leering and drooling at the new and improved version of their postmistress. Obviously Agnes, the town crier, had been hard at work.

Ralph Emmett, eighty years old if he was a day, was sprawled over the countertop, smiling a dopey smile up at Wendy. "Give me a one-cent stamp, will ya, sweetheart?"

Wendy, apparently having gotten the hang of her new shoes, carefully worked her way over to the drawer where she kept the one-centers. Bending low, she tore off one stamp and slowly made her way back to Ralph.

"Thanks, honey," he said, scratching his pendulous earlobes thoughtfully. "Come to think of it, I'm gonna need another one."

The "male" room collectively leaned forward as Wendy made her way back to the drawer and bent low to retrieve another one cent-stamp for Ralph.

Travis was annoyed. Didn't she realize that she was making a fool of herself? Not that he cared, mind you. Wendy was a big girl. She could handle herself. He hoped. If the wolfish expressions on half the town's male population were anything to judge by, he'd have to dig out his nail gun and start kickin' some stamp collecting butt.

"I sure like your new uniform," Ralph praised, figuring his two cents entitled him to share his opinion. "Especially them patches on the front. Them eagles make me proud to be an American." Doffing his hat, he shuffled off to the side to make way for Harold McCoy.

"Oh, you." Wendy flushed and ducked her head shyly. "How you do go on." Batting the crow's wings that clung to her bright blue eyelids, Travis couldn't be sure if she had something in her eye again or if she were awkwardly attempting to flirt with the curmudgeonly Ralph.

"You're looking mighty fine, Wendy," Harold assured her, and a murmur of elderly male voices echoed his sentiment. Leaning forward, he motioned for her to lend him her ear. "Is it true what they say?" he wanted to know in a stage whisper.

Her tentative frown was puzzled. "What do they say?"

Don't hurt her, Travis thought menacingly, and balled his fists at his sides.

"That blondes have more fun?"

Wendy glanced bashfully around the room, obviously taken aback by the uncommon and rather ardent siege of male attention. She lifted her shoulders lightly. "I don't know."

Shaking his head, Travis shuffled back to his work space and began setting up his table saw. He was going to have a hell of a time keeping a naive babe in the woods like her out of trouble.

Limping into the back room, Wendy headed toward the mini refrigerator that held her lunch. After she retrieved her brown bag and soda, she joined Travis at a table he'd fashioned from sawhorses and a sheet of plywood. The lobby crowd had finally abated and one of her part-time employees was manning the window. She groaned, a high-pitched gurgle in her throat, as she eased her aching body into a metal folding chair. Never before could she remember such a rush on one-cent stamps. It was amazing.

Longing for her practical, black, regulation postal shoes, she kicked off her high heels and rubbed her throbbing feet. She suddenly had a new and profound respect for BambiAnn. Walking in those meat-grinders day after day took a great deal of talent and mental fortitude.

Travis lifted his eyes from his copy of *Sports Illustrated* long enough to remove his thermos from his lunch pail. Then, seeming vaguely miffed about something, went back to his reading.

She wondered for a moment what his problem was, and if there was anything she could do to help. But, she decided, glancing around at the mess that littered her floor, she knew nothing about remodeling. Whatever was irritating him was out of her field of expertise. Deciding that maybe she could draw him out of his funk and into a conversation, she made up her mind to ask him a question that had puzzled her for three years now.

"Travis?" she asked, pulling her tuna fish on wheat bread out of her bag and opening the waxed paper that surrounded it.

"Hmm?"

Never one to mince words with her neighbor, she plunged in with both aching feet. "What ever happened to Dustin's mom?"

Travis groaned and dropped his arms over the top of his magazine. She could tell by the look on his face that he didn't enjoy talking about Elly Mae.

"I mean, I remember when she left and everything, but I never knew exactly why." Actually, Agnes, Minny and Ethel had loudly speculated on a number of theories, but none that Wendy had wanted to believe. "I've been curious about that lately."

"Why?" he grunted, and made himself busy by pouring a cup of coffee from his thermos.

"I just wondered what kind of woman you married. I'm kind of taking a survey, really. Trying to figure out what makes a man take the plunge." Looking hopefully up at him, she picked up her sandwich and held her breath.

"Aw, sheez." Travis shook his head and brought his coffee cup to his lips.

"Also," she pressed, playing her trump card, "I thought it could help me understand Dusty a little better."

Leaning on his elbows, Travis held his coffee cup between his two hands and eyed her over the rim. "Well," he began, and slowly lowered his cup to the table, "where do you want me to begin?"

"At the beginning."

He snorted. "We'll be here all night."

"I've got time," she encouraged quietly.

As Travis's eyes defocused and he proceeded to drift back in time, Wendy could hear Ralph Emmett back in the lobby, wondering when she'd be returning from her lunch break. Men were such funny creatures, she thought absently. Too bad old Ralph wasn't fifty years younger. He seemed downright captivated by her new look. However, urgent as things were, she wasn't that hard up. Cradling her face in her hand, she smiled softly and looked at her handsome neighbor. Too bad Dusty's dad wasn't more her type.

Running a finger along his lower lip, he exhaled mightily and sagged somewhat in his chair. "Elly Mae and I were high school sweethearts. Elly Mae Barston. Prettiest girl in New Hope."

Wendy nodded. She'd seen Dusty's beautiful mother.

Travis smiled in remembrance. "She was the homecoming queen and head pom-pom girl. I'm pretty sure Elly Mae was voted best-looking, most popular, most likely to succeed and, if I'm not mistaken," he said with a twinkle in his eye, "the cutest couple."

Wendy rolled her eyes.

"But then, you know I've always had a penchant for, uh, full-figured gals."

His eyes strayed to the peek a boo gap. Wendy felt her cheeks spontaneously combust and bit into her sandwich to hide her discomfiture.

"Anyway, we were quite the pair. Me in my New Hope High Jackrabbit football uniform—"

"*Jackrabbit?*" Wendy interrupted, choking on her tuna and whole wheat. "The high school football team is the *Jackrabbits?* I never knew that." Leaning back in her chair, she lifted her aching feet up onto the makeshift table and laughed until her eyeliner began to run. "Oh," she gasped, carefully dabbing at the blackish tears with her napkin. "I can see why Elly Mae couldn't resist you in a Jackrabbit outfit."

Giving her brightly painted toes a playful shake, he narrowed his eyes in mock outrage. "Hey, we were fast."

"I'll bet." Wendy giggled. "Among other things."

Travis's eyes traveled from her toes to her nicely turned ankles, then slowly skimmed her shapely calves, knees and thighs. "And," he said, his voice low with innuendo, "here I thought you were such an innocent."

Squinting, Wendy wadded her waxed paper and lobbed it at his head. "Get back to the story," she ordered, reaching into her bag for a carrot stick.

He dragged his eyes away from her legs and did her bidding. "Okay, let's see ... After high school, Elly Mae had a hard time keeping a job. I think I've finally figured out that she was one of those people where high school is the highlight of their life. In real life, she couldn't skate along on her looks, and nobody wanted to pay her to be homecoming queen or head pom-pom girl. So she stayed home and started watching soap operas. I think she found an escape there, because she became addicted to them. Began to pattern her life after them. I didn't know it, of course, because I was busy learning the building construction trade and taking college business courses at night."

Wendy stretched and nodded thoughtfully.

Reaching over, Travis snitched a carrot stick from her bag and thoughtfully crunched it for a moment. "Anyway," he continued. "Her favorite soap was Restless Hospital. And her favorite character was Daisy Knights. I think Elly Mae longed for the exciting and glamorous life that Daisy led. Kind of like the life Elly Mae led in high school."

"Makes sense," Wendy murmured, amazed at Travis's ability to speak so objectively when it came to his ex-wife. She admired the way he'd analyzed and then accepted Elly Mae's needs.

"So, Elly Mae began to pattern her life after Daisy Knights. When Daisy got married, Elly Mae got married. When Daisy had a baby, Elly Mae had a baby. And when

Daisy had a nervous breakdown, changed her name to Day, and decided to chuck it all and run off with another man...." Travis's light gray eyes flitted to hers, then back down to his hands. "Well, you get the idea."

Wendy nodded empathetically. "I'm so sorry," she murmured. And she was. Sorry for him. Sorry for the woman who would miss out on the pleasure of growing old with the rascal who sat across from her. But, most of all, sorry for the little boy, still soft with baby fat, who longed for a mother's love.

"Don't be," Travis mumbled around a mouthful of her potato chips. "I'm over it." His grin was resigned. "Elly Mae changed her name to Elle, and moved with her new rich husband to upstate New York. Thankfully, she left me with full custody of Dustin. Said mothering wasn't her thing."

This time Wendy dabbed at her eyes, but it wasn't out of laughter. Sometimes life could be so cruel. Travis's story had given her a whole new understanding of him and the way he was now with women. She understood his comment about the men on her list being wealthy. She could see that he'd been hurt. Badly hurt. And he was retaliating, the only way he knew how. For some reason she felt much closer to Dustin Donovan's dad. Perhaps, she mused, it was because of the intimate nature of their conversation. Or perhaps it was the way he kept raking his eyes across her legs. In any event, she could feel an almost palpable kinship with him. He was hiding behind the persona he'd invented to protect himself from getting hurt, much the way she had. Deep down, they weren't so different, really.

Outside, the community church chimed the hour. Wendy knew that she'd better get back out front to Ralph Emmett and the other townspeople who'd be looking for their stamps and checking to see if Agnes had been telling the truth.

With a heartfelt groan, Wendy lifted her feet off the table where they'd been recuperating, and stuffed them, blisters and all, into her new four-inch-high platforms. It was going to be a long damn day.

4

After work that evening Wendy burst through the front door of her house and made her way back to her bedroom, shedding her torturous man-catcher getup as she went. Good golly Almighty, why did women have to put themselves through all this rigmarole just to catch a man? It was all so silly, she thought, kicking her shoes off as she unbuttoned her postal halter top. Oh, she couldn't wait to get this horrible underwire push-up bra off. The stupid thing had more metal than a bird cage.

Wendy didn't think Travis would ever consider putting himself through this much pain just to impress BambiAnn. Yet, she knew that poor girl regularly squeezed herself into unnaturally tight outfits that would surely do terrible damage to her major internal organs one day.

It was scary, Wendy thought as she twisted and turned, struggling with her newfangled bra. She was really beginning to sympathize with little ol' BambiAnn. She had to give the woman credit. This catching-a-man business was hell.

Moving over to the mirror, Wendy held her breath and winced in pain as she stripped off her false eyelashes. Next, off came the dangling earrings, hair barrettes and bows, and other costume jewelry from around her neck and wrists. After smearing a layer of Phase I facial cleanser onto her face, she turned on the shower and once the temperature was right, stepped into the hot, steamy spray, and relaxed.

Oh, heavens to mergatroid, she'd never enjoyed a shower this much before in her life. She shampooed her hair with Sue Ellen's special split-end-healing concoction, then conditioned it with the honey-lemon-avocado-mayonnaise mess that Sue Ellen had assured her would leave her hair soft and manageable. Wendy didn't know about that, but if it didn't work on her hair, it would probably taste pretty good on a salad.

Steam filled the bathroom as she stepped out of the shower and made her way back to the foggy mirror. Toweling off a spot, she looked at her face, squeaky-clean now, and began to realize just how childlike she looked without all the Mabel Lee makeup. She glanced at the clock.

There was no time for the full regalia if she was going to make it over to Travis's house by seven for the first dating lesson. Deciding to skip the false eyelashes and heavy blue eye shadow, Wendy quickly applied a sheer layer of base, some powder for her nose and cheeks, a little mascara—which was trickier stuff than she'd ever imagined—and some pale lipstick. There, she thought with a tiny frown. It wasn't the full-blown man-catching beauty regime, but then again, the only men she would be seeing tonight were Dusty and Travis and they didn't really count.

Dragging a comb through her permanent wave, she decided against the mousse and styling gel, as well, and after a quick blow-dry, caught her hair at the back of head in a loose ponytail of honey-streaked, sun-blond-goddess waves. Then to her closet. There, the only halfway decent clothes she could find to learn to dance in were a pair of jeans, so tight she had to lie on her back to zip them up, and an oversize short sweatshirt with a ripped-off collar and three-quarter sleeves.

Once she'd struggled her way into her designer jeans, she held the sweatshirt up and marveled at how she'd been talked into spending sixty dollars on it. What on earth had she been thinking? she wondered, stretching it on over her head. Especially since the stupid thing kept slipping off her shoulder that way. It was darn lucky she'd stayed as fit as possible. As it was, she was practically bursting out of these silly jeans. Oh, well. Beth had assured her that this was what she'd need to snare a man. All the guys just loved this look, the young girl had promised.

Sighing, Wendy grabbed her hundred-and-fifty-dollar cross-trainer tennis shoes and a pair of aerobic sweat socks and headed across the driveway to Travis.

For a brief moment Travis didn't recognize the babe on his doorstep who stood smiling up at him with her bright, aquamarine eyes.

"Are you ready?" she asked, breezing past him, her tennis shoes slung casually over her shoulder.

Travis blinked. *Wendy?* He was surely seeing things. This cute little package with the jeans that hugged her delectable little derriere was *Wendy?* Damnation! If he hadn't known she was coming over, he'd never have guessed. She looked wonderful! Cute enough to grace the cover of that *Metropolitan* magazine any day, in his opinion.

Reaching into her pup-tent-size purse, she withdrew several compact discs. "Beth loaned me these rock-and-roll albums by some of the hot new bands," she said, holding up the CDs. "She says these guys are hot, hot, hot, so I figured you could teach me to fast dance to them. And slow dance, too," she informed him, and pitched her purse into his hall closet. "I'll need to know that." Kicking the bag all the way inside, she slammed the closet door and turned to face him. "Plus, I've never been one of those hothouse flowers who needed help opening the dang door. But since men seem to like doing those things, I guess I could put up with it." Grinning, she planted her knuckles on her hips. "So, it would help if you could tell me what you like in the way of helping a woman into the car, or seating her in the restaurant and, you know, when opening a door—"

Travis nodded, tuning her out as she listed her demands for lesson number one. He was still unable to believe the transformation that had taken place in her look. She didn't seem the least bit aware of how different she looked. How beautiful, really. It was uncanny. The same voice was coming out of the same mouth saying the same bossy things the same as usual. But the trouble was, she wasn't the same anymore. Not at all. At least, not on the outside. She was cute. Really cute. And, being the man that he was, he found himself reacting to her new look on a purely animal level.

He shook his head to clear it. Good grief. What the hell was he doing here? This was *Wendy*. Wendy. Neighbor. Playmate to Dustin. Postmistress. Ugly-shoe owner. Buddy. Nothing more. Nothing less.

Get a handle on it, man, he warned himself.

"Also, I've been thinking that you need to coach me how to make small talk. I feel like such a boob and get all tongue-tied whenever I have to talk to a really handsome man, so..." She paused for air, then, turning toward his living room continued her enthusiastic diatribe.

Something suddenly rankled, and Travis couldn't quite put his finger on it. He followed her toward his living room wondering what had put the nasty, gnawing, almost hurt feeling in his gut, when it dawned on him.

She'd said she had problems talking to really handsome men.

Plowing a hand through his thick, brown hair, he listened to her yabber her head off and wondered what that made him. Something she'd stepped on out in the yard? Hell, he'd never had any trouble attracting a woman's attention before. Criminy sakes, he had them hanging all over him every Friday night down at Little Joe's Café. She could just ask Sue Ellen, if she didn't believe him, he thought huffily. Sue Ellen practically owned the damn place. She'd know.

Sheesh. What a head case he was becoming. She goes and dyes her hair and suddenly it's important what she thinks of him. How idiotic. He'd given up worrying about what women thought of him when Elly Mae took off. Heck, he didn't even care if BambiAnn thought he was handsome. So why should he care if the wallflower next door thought so or not?

She had turned and was looking up at him. "So. Think that's doable for lesson number one?" Smiling winsomely, she dropped to his couch and began stuffing her brightly painted toes into her socks and shoes.

Aw, man. Even her feet were cute. He thought about suggesting that she go put on a pair of her giant, black, postal clodhoppers, but remembered her telling him that she'd given them to charity. Damn.

Travis cleared his throat. "Uh, yeah," he finally managed. "I think we can get a lot of it done."

"Great," Wendy grunted as she finished tying her shoes and then bounded to her feet. She glanced around the house. "Where's Dusty?"

"Taking a bath. He'll play in there for a while and leave us alone. He's got the fleet out, so we have at least half an hour to get started. So. Uh. What should we do first?" he asked, feeling strangely shy. He was feeling shy? He hadn't felt like this since he and Elly Mae had shared their first kiss under the Jackrabbit bleachers down at New Hope High.

Wendy, however, did not seem the least bit reticent about her impending lessons, he thought grumpily. As far as she was concerned, he was just an object. A nonentity. Simply there to take her from crayons to perfume.

Oh, so what. He had to get over himself if he was going to make it through the evening. Taking a stoic breath, he squared his shoulders and prepared himself mentally as she opened the doors to his entertainment center.

Squinting thoughtfully at his stereo, she hit the power button and, whipping a CD out of its case, slid it into the player. "Let's get the dancing out of the way, while the night is still young," she suggested over her shoulder, and adjusted the volume on the pulsing, throbbing rhythm that vibrated from his stereo speakers.

"Okay." He nodded, moving the coffee table and an armchair out of the middle of his large, simply furnished living room. Dancing was something he was pretty good at. Listening to the pounding beat of the latest sound, a feeling of buoyancy overtook him. This might be kind of fun. Who'd have ever thought it? he wondered, shrugging good-naturedly. Teaching good ol' Wendy next door to dance. How about that. He passed a hand over his jaw. If only it were still that simple. "Now, then," he said, pulling her into the middle of the room. "What you have to do first, is relax." Giving her bare shoulder an encouraging squeeze, he couldn't help but notice how incredibly soft her skin was. "Then," he continued before he had time to analyze the soft-shoulder issue, "you just let yourself feel the music. Listen."

Closing her eyes, Wendy dropped her shoulders and listened. Her pale pink lips puckered thoughtfully.

Travis stifled a groan. "Next, the most important thing about this kind of dancing is doing what makes you feel comfortable. Anything goes, really, but several things are universal."

Opening her eyes, she watched him intently as he began to move. "Like what?" she wondered out loud.

"Like moving your hips. Like this," he said, and demonstrated, setting his jeans-clad tush into motion.

"Oh . . ." she breathed, her eyes widening.

"Then, of course, you have to move your hands back and forth, like this . . ." He raised his arms over his head, snapping his fingers to the beat. "Or like this . . ." He swung them back and forth, displaying yet another move. "Or, you know, pretty much anything you want to do, like this." He began to move around her in a circle, occasionally bumping her hip with his, nudging her into gear.

Wendy began to move, her motions were tight and stilted from complete lack of experience. Not to mention the fact that she found the whole process completely ludicrous. What in heaven's name good did all of these gyrations do? Would this really help her snare a husband? She sighed. It was all so silly. Well, if it would land her a life partner, she guessed she'd better "swang her thang."

"Come on," Travis urged, seeming to get into the spirit of the lesson. He reached out and took her by the hands, pulling her around the oval throw rug on his floor. "Loosen up."

"But," she protested, stumbling along beside him, "there doesn't seem to be any rhyme or reason to any of the steps you're doing. I mean, at least when you're waltzing or fox-trotting, there are some basic steps to follow."

"Yeah," Travis agreed, snapping his fingers and clapping his hands and spinning in happy circles. "But in a way, that's the beauty of it. It's kind of like making love. Anything goes." He nudged her with his behind, knocking her off balance.

Taking a steadying step, Wendy rolled her eyes. "I hope that's not on tonight's agenda."

"Well," Travis grinned devilishly, "maybe I could give you some advice in that department if you're rusty."

"No, thank you," she said primly as her entire head went pink.

Travis guffawed good-naturedly and proceeded to bump and grind his way around her, clapping his hands over his head, all the while staring down into her eyes.

Wendy flashed a glance down at her expensive tennis shoes and willed them to dance. Oh, yeah. She was rusty, all right. If never having had a physical relationship of any kind with a man meant rusty, then she was a regular tin woodsman. Heavens. Much to her eternal mortification, she'd only gotten one good-night kiss in her entire dating career and that had been on the cheek.

However, that wasn't surprising, considering the way her mother would barge out to the front porch the moment one of her brave young suitors had walked her to the door. No wonder sister Wanda had climbed out the window every night to escape their mother's watchful eye.

And though she had no intention of taking Travis up on his ridiculous offer, she couldn't help but wonder what it would be like being married to him. Waking up with him. Sharing Dusty with him. She shook her head. What on earth was she thinking? This was *Travis,* for pity's sake! Good old devil-may-care Travis.

"Look at me," he ordered. "That's part of the whole deal. Eye contact." Taking her hands in his, he looped them around his neck and then circled her waist with his arms. He leaned his forehead against hers and stared deeply into her eyes. "I never noticed how blue your eyes are," he said, wonder filling his voice.

"That's because they're not," Wendy said, nervously wetting her lower lip with her tongue. She'd been doing just fine until this move. How would she ever learn to relax with a man when he held her this close? This whole touching deal was completely out of her realm of experience. It was a good thing she was getting the jitters out of the way with Travis. Because it certainly wouldn't do to sweat this profusely with a prospective husband. "I, um," she stammered, trying like the dickens to sustain eye contact. It was harder than she'd ever dreamed. Although, not in an altogether disagreeable way, really. In fact, with some more practice, she might even come to enjoy it. Look forward to it.

She could see the tiny flecks of gold and green in his gray eyes. "I'm wearing colored contacts. Actually, my eyes are brown. Like my hair."

"Oh. No wonder I never noticed before." He winked teasingly at her.

Blessedly, he pulled her arms from around his neck and proceeded to teach her how to follow her partner around the room. The steady pulse of the drums and the heavy tones of the bass guitar finally began to work their magic. Before she knew it, Wendy was beginning to relax and enjoy the art of the fast dance.

"Here." His silky voice came to her from just over her shoulder as he laid his hands on either side of her hips. "Like this," he urged, moving her hips in a circle until she began to get the hang of it. "Good," he praised, and began to move with her. "Real good." His sexy tone held a note that Wendy had never heard before.

"Hey, whatcha guys doin'?" Dusty shrieked, galloping into the living room, wearing nothing but a towel clutched loosely at his waist.

They sprang guiltily apart at the child's giggling voice, and avoided each other's eyes.

"Hey, sweet potato!" Wendy called to the exuberant boy as he stumbled and slipped down the hallway toward her. "We were dancing."

"Dancing?" Dustin shouted, reaching the living room. "Oh, boy!" Loosing control of his towel, it slid down his bare bottom while he jumped around the room to the raucous rock.

Wendy took one look at the bare cheeks as they bounced to the beat of the music and felt the mirth well into her throat. "So—" she looked over at Travis and laughed "—that's what I've been doing wrong."

Travis raised a playful eye. "Oh. Did I neglect to mention the part about dropping your drawers?" He turned and addressed his son. "Dusty, where's your modesty?"

"Just a minute, Dad," he yelped, jumping off the couch. Stumbling over his towel, he rolled around on the floor. "I'll go get it."

Wendy and Travis stood together, watching his antics till the end of the song, both aware that things had begun to change between them just before the young boy had arrived. It was a good thing he'd come in when he had. This was a platonic relationship for heaven's sake, they thought, not daring to look at each other. After all, they thought, *Wendy? Travis?* Come on. Get real. Shaking their heads to clear the temporary insanity, they found each other's eyes.

"I think it's time for a break," Travis suggested, his gaze tangling with hers.

"Yes," she murmured, backing up and switching off the stereo. "How about some chocolate milk, kiddo?" Wendy asked, reaching for Dustin's hand.

"Yeah!" he shouted gleefully.

"But first, why don't we go find your pajamas?"

"Aw..."

Travis watched them go—hand in hand toward his son's bedroom, Dusty's little bottom still hanging out of his towel, hers still packed fetchingly in those damnably tight jeans. And once again he experienced a growing pain somewhere in the vicinity of his shriveled and broken heart.

Dustin fell asleep as Wendy was reading the requested bedtime story. She leaned over and kissed his soft cheek. Stroking his golden hair away from his brow, she smiled down at the sweet expression on his young face. Someday soon, if she was lucky, she would have a little boy to call her own. A little boy just half as wonderful as Dusty would make her happier than she'd ever dreamed possible.

He was the reason, really, for her current husband quest. Until she'd fallen blissfully in love with the little bundle of energy next door, she'd never known what she'd been missing. Never known just how much she craved the grubby kisses and affectionate face pats that only a five-year-old could bestow. Never known how a simple Halloween costume could take on an entirely different meaning when viewed through a child's eyes. And never known how desperately she'd needed to be loved herself. She had Dusty to thank for waking her up. Him, and the magazine article she'd found in the recycling bin.

As she smoothed the covers up beneath the young boy's chin, Wendy sensed Travis's presence in the doorway, and wondered just how long he'd been standing there, watching. She turned, caught his eye and saw there a look of sweet poignancy, as his gaze traveled from her to his son.

Running his hand across the back of his neck, he breathed deeply and smiled at her. "He adores you, you know."

Angling her head toward him, Wendy returned his soft smile. "Ah, yes. But I'm afraid only half as much as I adore him."

Travis nodded, as if he understood the depth of the relationship that had formed between her and his son from the time Dusty was no more than a toddler. She knew Travis realized she was really the only constant, loving maternal figure the boy had ever had. Not wanting to rouse the sleeping cherub at her side, she carefully stood and after Travis had laid a gentle kiss of his own on the boy's cheek, followed him back to the living room to resume their lessons.

"Melvin-Jasper?" Wendy squealed, sticking her finger down her throat and pretending to gag. "You can't be serious."

They were sitting together on his couch, drinking ice tea and going over the list of eligible bachelors that Travis had prepared for her.

Soft country music was now playing on the stereo, after they'd abandoned the slow-dance lessons. Travis told her he had to stop because the tops of his feet couldn't take any more punishment, but in actuality, it was his libido that had taken the bashing. It just felt too damn weird, holding the New Hope postmistress that close. It was almost as if he was putting a move on the local schoolmarm or something equally kinky and taboo.

So, he'd dropped her like a hot potato and run to the freezer to fish out a tray of ice for the tea, and of course, to cool down his increasingly bizarre reaction to the prim and proper postal worker from next door.

"What's wrong with Melvin-Jasper?" he asked, leaning back to look curiously at her.

"No way!" She giggled. "I get mooned every time he bends over. What's with his pants, anyway? Can't you go in with some of the guys on your crew and get him a pair of suspenders or something?"

Travis sent her a wounded look. "You didn't seem to mind being in his company when he was on our bowling team last fall," he said, defending the rough-around-the-edges Melvin-Jasper.

"True." She pulled a thoughtful face. "And I must admit I found it fascinating that anyone could bowl at all with their pants down around their knees that way, let alone score so consistently high. So—" she glanced up at him "—you think Melvin-Jasper would make me a good husband, huh?"

Travis pinched his upper lip between his thumb and forefinger, looking askance at her. No. It was true. He couldn't really see the two of them making a life together. Though Melvin-Jasper—when he wasn't spitting tobacco juice all over the floor—was a great guy, it was really no surprise that he hadn't found a wife. Travis figured that it would take a pretty special woman to put up with Melvin-Jasper's particular brand of body odor. Melvin-Jasper wasn't much for dallying in the shower. "Okay, cross him off."

With a vigorous scribble, Wendy did just that. "Let's see now, who else have you got up your sleeve?" she murmured, perusing his list.

"I put down every unmarried guy I could think of," Travis said, scooting closer to her on the sofa so that he could read over her shoulder. She sure smelled good. Whatever Sue Ellen had told her to dab on her neck was light and feminine and smelled sort of like a big bunch of flowers. Made him want to bury his nose in her neck. He reared back as she looked up and squinted at him.

"Jake Spencer?"

"What's wrong with Jake Spencer?"

She looked back down at the note in her hands. "Travis, what rock have you been living under? Jake Spencer and Pricilla Barrington are getting married sometime soon. Priss is expecting a baby." Leaning toward him, she pointed at the list. "The same thing with Mitch McCord. He and Jenny Stevens got together a few months ago." She threw her hands up in exasperation. "See! I told you there are no men left for me." She looked up at him, her eyes wide with worry.

"Hey, now," he said, snatching the note out of her hands. "There must be one or two people on this list who aren't attached. Okay. These three right here." He held the paper up for her inspection. "These three guys happen to work for me. And I know for a fact that none of them is married."

"Hmm." She hummed and narrowed her eyes. "I'll check the Wanted posters for their names."

"Very funny."

"Well, forgive me for not exactly trusting your instincts when it comes to finding me a husband. I mean, come on, Jake? Mitch?"

"How did you know the lowdown on those guys? I mean, for crying out loud, I play poker with them, and I didn't even know. Didn't even have a chance to talk some sense into them." He shook his head morosely.

"When was the last time you guys played poker?"

"Last spring, I guess."

"Ah, well, if you want to keep up on the local goings-on, you have to get the scoop from Agnes and the gang down at the post office." Her eyes darkened with concern. "You really would have tried to talk them out of getting married?"

He shrugged.

"You're still pretty bitter about Elly Mae."

Travis glanced down the hall toward his son's room. "She didn't hurt just me."

"I know," she whispered.

"You're still serious about this whole husband-hunting business, huh?"

She nodded. "I have to try."

He rubbed his jaw. "I sure hope you don't end up regretting this harebrained idea."

"I promise to learn from your mistakes."

Reaching out, he touched her chin with his fingertip. "I hope you don't have to."

They sat for a moment, each thinking their private thoughts, until the grandfather clock in the family room chimed the hour.

"Midnight?" Wendy asked, surprised. "I have to get going. I have to get up at the crack of dawn tomorrow. It takes forever and a day to do my hair and put on my makeup the way Sue Ellen showed me. I don't know how she does it."

"I don't know *why* she does it," Travis murmured.

"Because it makes her beautiful," she explained. "Like BambiAnn."

"If you say so."

She arched a quizzical brow. Why would he make a comment like that? Didn't all men want their women to look their best? Maybe he and BambiAnn had had a tiff. At any rate, she wouldn't worry about Travis's opinion. He wasn't the one she was trying to impress.

"You want to carpool again tomorrow?" he asked, changing the subject.

"Great." She grinned. "I promise I'll walk to the car by myself and everything."

"I don't know. Dusty loved how you flew down the stairs. He was convinced that you did it on purpose." Travis laughed and squeezed her shoulder. Again, he was struck by its softness. "We should probably go out on a practice date pretty soon," he suggested.

"Okay. How about day after tomorrow?"

"Wednesday? I think I'm free." His grin was self-deprecating.

"Great. I'll talk to Faith during my lunch break tomorrow about watching Dusty on Wednesday night. Now that she's expecting a baby of her own, maybe she could use the practice taking care of a child." Standing, she headed toward the hall closet to gather her purse.

Travis nodded and followed her to the door. "Good idea." There was an awkward moment before she moved down the steps and they waved goodbye to each other.

"'Bye," she called cheerfully.

"'Bye," he returned softly, and waited on his porch until she made it safely inside her house. He didn't move until the light had gone out in her bedroom.

The bell above the door at the Baby Boutique whispered a baby-soft greeting as Wendy entered the foreign world she longed to someday become a part of. Teddy bears and dolls, mobiles and bumper pads, cribs, strollers and high chairs filled virtually every nook and cranny. Something about just walking through the door made her ache for a child of her own. The Baby Boutique even smelled like a baby. Fresh and new, and a little like baby powder and lotion.

Faith Harper looked up from where she stood behind the counter and smiled broadly at Wendy. Wendy felt something of a sister kinship with Faith that she didn't feel with her own sister. Slender, long, light brown hair, and well liked by Agnes and the gang, Faith had always been just about as prim and proper as they come.... That is, until she'd turned up pregnant almost eight months ago. Add to that the fact that Faith wouldn't say one word about who the father of the baby was and, well, New Hope, Texas, hadn't had so much to speculate upon in years.

Until, of course, Wendy had shocked them all out of their minds with her new look yesterday. The phone lines last night had been abuzz—possibly smoking at Agnes's house—with the delicious story of her husband hunt. Why, today Agnes, Minny and Ethel had even stormed into the post office lobby and proclaimed loudly that Wendy Wilcox would surely go to the devil if she didn't mend her ways. More than ever, she could sympathize with Faith.

"Hi, Wendy," Faith called as her friend wove her way toward the counter. "I love your new look. It must be so nice to have a tiny waist like yours," she said, her voice wistful.

"Hi, Faith," Wendy said, smiling. "I think you're the one who's looking beautiful."

"Ugh." Faith rolled her eyes and smiled down at her burgeoning midsection. "I just wish it was over with."

"Are you ready?" Wendy asked, then laughed and looked around. "I guess that was a dumb question. You must have everything you need."

Faith nodded and looked at her hands. "I guess..."

Darn, Wendy thought. *That was dumb.* Obviously she doesn't have the father of the baby. That must be rough. Silently berating herself for her faux pas, Wendy decided to change the subject. "Well, I just hope you can make it to the Russo wedding next month. It's the big social event of the season. Aside from the engagement party you threw for Michael and Michelle last February, of course," she said, and grinned at Faith who drew her lower lip between her teeth.

"Actually," Wendy continued, "that's the reason... I'm... here..." Wendy's voice trailed off in concern as a look of pain flashed across Faith's face. "Oh, honey. Are you going to be okay?" Wendy stood uncertainly, wondering what to do. She'd never spent much time in the company of a pregnant woman. What were the first signs of labor, anyway?

"I'm okay," Faith said, smiling wanly. "Just a little in digestion."

"Are you sure?" Wendy could boil water with the best of them, but she'd rather not, if she didn't have to. She'd never understood what all the boiling water was for anyway. Surely it wasn't used on the baby or the mother...

"I'm sure." Faith nodded. "I'm sorry. I didn't mean to interrupt. You were saying?"

"Oh. Yes." Wendy leaned a hip against the counter to rest her foot. Again, her feet were killing her. "Well, as I'm sure you've heard by now, I'm husband hunting."

Faith's lips quirked up at the corners. "Agnes may have mentioned..."

Wendy grinned. "Oh, it's okay. It's no secret. Everyone's been just great about helping. Sue Ellen did my hair and makeup, and Beth remodeled my uniform..." She batted her false eyelashes and pointed at the peek a boo hole. "Personally, I think they went slightly overboard. But, hey, they promise results, so who am I?" She laughed easily, her giant sun-goddess corkscrews dancing and swaying at wild right angles. "Anyway, Travis Donovan, you know him—my neighbor? He's giving me lessons on, you know, dating etiquette and such. I, uh, didn't get much experience in my youth," she admitted, blushing.

"Don't feel bad, Wendy. Neither did I." Faith reached out and squeezed Wendy's hand.

Wendy knew if she confided in Faith, her friend would be supportive and wonderful. A sudden lump gathered in her throat. The people in this town were just so darn nice. Even Agnes and the gang had only her best interests at heart.

Blinking rapidly, she returned the squeeze to Faith's hand. "Anyway, Travis and I were wondering if you'd mind watching Dusty tomorrow night so that we could go out on a 'practice date.' Normally, I wouldn't ask, but we figured maybe you could use the practice yourself since you were expecting your own little bundle of energy soon."

Faith's head bobbed thoughtfully. "Wednesday evening? I don't think I have anything planned. I'd love to do my part to help you get your man, Wendy." Absently, she rubbed the bare spot on her own ring finger.

Wendy's sigh of relief was audible. "Thanks, Faith, you're a peach. I've got to get over to the diner to see if Sue Ellen can come over tomorrow night and help me put my hair up for my date. Then I've got to get back to the post office. It's been unusually busy there lately." She frowned. "I'm selling one-cent stamps like there's no tomorrow. Anyway—" she smiled at Faith "—Travis will bring you over to our place after work. His, I mean. His place. We're carpooling this week. Thanks so much for this."

Faith tenderly patted the baby beneath her breast. "Oh, don't thank me yet. I have a feeling you may be returning the favor one of these days." She smiled as Wendy tottered unsteadily toward the door on her new high heels.

The soft bell announced her departure. "I'd love that," Wendy said, clutching the front door to keep from falling over. "I'll see you tomorrow night."

5

Wendy stared, unseeing, down the drain of her bathroom sink. Moments before she'd been rinsing and cleaning her bright blue aquamarine contact lenses. Now they were enjoying the interior view of her plumbing as they made their way toward the New Hope sewage treatment plant.

Don't panic, she sternly warned herself, taking deep, fortifying breaths of air. What, in heaven's name, had possessed her to put her old glasses in the charity bag? Hour Optical wouldn't open again until tomorrow morning, so, until then, she was stuck.

Why, Lord? Why me? Moaning, she squinted at the clock on the wall and tried desperately to make out the position of the fuzzy hands. It appeared, as far as she could tell, that she had just over an hour to finish getting ready. And, of course now that she was nearly legally blind, the process would probably take a lot longer. It was a good thing Sue Ellen would be doing her hair for the evening.

Thankfully, this wasn't a real date. Just a practice session with Travis. Still and all, she wanted to make it as authentic as possible, and that included dressing up for the occasion.

The doorbell chimed. Must be Sue Ellen, Wendy thought, tightening the sash to her bathrobe. She clutched the door frame until she could find her balance on the new, shiny gold, open-toed, high-heeled sandals that graced her feet.

Groping along the hallway, she followed the insistent sound as Sue Ellen leaned impatiently on the bell.

"I'm coming," she called, and could only pray that it were true and that she was indeed heading in the right direction. Finding the doorknob to the big, dark fuzzy blob that was her front door, she pulled it open to be greeted by the vague image of very large blond hair and a well-padded hourglass figure.

"Sue Ellen?"

"Yes, honey, it's me," Sue Ellen grunted, dragging several suitcases of beauty paraphernalia behind her into Wendy's house. Unceremoniously dumping the luggage in her living room, the flamboyant woman exhaled loudly with relief. Turning, she watched as Wendy felt her way along the wall. "Honey, what's the matter with you?"

"I dropped my contacts down the drain," Wendy moaned, tears welling in her eyes. "I can't see a darn thing without them."

"Where are your old glasses? I'll get 'em for you," Sue Ellen volunteered helpfully.

Wendy found her couch and slumped into a pitiful heap. "Like an idiot, I gave them to charity."

"And you don't have another pair?" Sue Ellen asked, concerned.

"No." Wendy pulled her head out of her hands and sighed. "Not yet."

"Are you nearsighted or farsighted?"

"Nearsighted." Wendy frowned. "Why?"

"Me, too," Sue Ellen muttered as she grabbed her large purse and dove headfirst—big hair and all—into its depths. "And... you know, I think I have an old pair of prescription sunglasses in here somewhere."

Her voice was muffled as she tossed various and sundry obstructions to her search onto the floor. A hair-dryer, cell phone, tennis shoe, tennis ball, a bag of candy kisses and a bowling trophy all hit the floor.

"The glasses are really old and kind of scratched up, but at least they could help you see a little better, couldn't they? We can't have you stumbling around blind all evening," Sue Ellen mumbled as she continued her rummaging.

"No?" Wendy warbled. She had half a mind to call Travis and call off the whole ordeal. She'd waited this long to try the dating scene again. Putting it off a few more days shouldn't matter, should it? Visions of her thirtieth birthday loomed blurrily on the horizon. No. She had to go through with it. She was running out of time.

"Eureka!" Sue Ellen finally shouted, holding up her discovery. "Here you go." She opened the plastic-and-wire, cat's-eye-style glasses and perched them on the tip of Wendy's nose.

Wendy blinked as the world slowly came into a fuzzy dark green focus. It was true. She could see a little better. *Little* being the operative word.

"Thanks, Sue Ellen. At least now I can find my way down the hall without killing myself." Smiling, she stood and abruptly stumbled over Sue Ellen's bowling trophy.

Luckily, Sue Ellen had lightning-fast reflexes and managed to catch her before she crumpled to the floor. "You okay, hon?"

"Yes, thanks." Wendy giggled as she righted herself and squinted into the dim green of her hallway.

Gracious, she was a nervous wreck. Why on earth should she be so uptight about a simple evening out on the town with Travis? she wondered, wiping her damp palms on her old chenille robe. If there was anyone she was *not* worried about impressing, it was him.

Perhaps it was just the idea of finally going out on a date after all these years. She would be a bit of a fish out of water, trying to make witty small talk and flirt and bat her eyes like BambiAnn, and . . . golly, the myriad things she would have to practice tonight if she was going accomplish her mission. How would she remember it all?

In her mind, it was almost as if this test date with Travis would be indicative of her future success. But that was ridiculous, she chided herself. How could a date with the playboy next door be any indication of how a real evening would go once she found a suitable suitor?

Relax! she commanded herself. This evening was just a trial run. A little icebreaker. Something to help her get her feet wet.

Wendy waited for Sue Ellen to gather her curious cosmetic bags, then slowly led the way back to her bathroom.

Once they arrived in her spacious, modern bath, Sue Ellen began to unpack. "You know, I forgot I even had those sunglasses," she said, peering at Wendy's reflection in the bathroom mirror. "They're a little bit out of style, but, hey, in a pinch they'll do the trick, huh?"

Wendy nodded. Personally, she thought they were even uglier than her old glasses, but Sue Ellen had a point. "Sure," she agreed, tearing her eyes away from her reflection and rotating her shoulders to help ease the nervous tension. *Calm down, calm down,* she chanted silently. This is just a simple evening with good old Travis. This is not the real thing. No need to let something like... not being able to see, worry her. Besides, it wasn't as if she cared what Travis thought of her inability to see, or her lack of experience with men. Luckily, he accepted her just the way she was. If she came off a little half-baked tonight, no matter. Her pal Travis probably wouldn't even notice.

So, why the frayed nerves? Must be that she wanted to show Travis that she wasn't a total dud in the dating department. After all, she had her pride, too. Wendy filled her lungs with cleansing oxygen and, ever so slowly, her roiling insides began to quiet.

"Go ahead and sit down," Sue Ellen instructed, gesturing to the small vanity stool. She glanced at her watch. "We don't have much time, so we'd better step on it."

"It's okay, Sue Ellen," Wendy said, finally accepting the fact that she wasn't going to be able to see much of anything until tomorrow morning. "It's just Travis. He won't care if I'm a little late."

"Well, we don't want to keep him waiting too long. Just long enough to be fashionable," Sue Ellen said, imparting yet another of her pearls of dating wisdom. After plugging in the hot rollers, the older woman began unpacking a small cooler filled with fresh-cut flowers. "Thought I'd try something special for your first date," she said, sticking large stalks of gladiolus and daisies into the sink and turning on the water. Snapping several small pieces of baby's breath off a larger bunch, Sue Ellen chattered a mile a minute while Wendy looked on—the best she could—in fascination.

Wow. She'd never have thought of putting fresh flowers in her hair. Is that what men liked? What funny creatures they were, she thought, giving her head a slight shake as Sue Ellen loaded her honey-streaked, sun-blond-goddess tresses with the now scalding-hot rollers. Wendy's head began to feel like boiled lobster. A curly, boiled lobster.

Sue Ellen fluffed and teased, spritzed and back-combed, hummed and flower arranged. "Take a deep breath and hold," the beauty school dropout instructed as she applied a heavy mist of hair spray. "You know, I have a new blusher I want to try on you. It has little sparkles in it. For that luminous look. And I brought along some different eye shadows I want to test," she continued, jabbering away as she worked.

Thirty minutes later Sue Ellen finally handed Wendy the cat's-eye sunglasses and told her to take a peek.

Slowly, Wendy pushed the glasses up on her nose and her dark green image came into semifocus. Her heart leapt into her throat. As far as she could tell, her hair was now upswept into one of the most amazing floral displays she'd ever laid two blurry eyes on. She'd seen bridal bouquets with less fanfare. Ribbons and curls and baby's breath and daisies and gladiolus and . . . oh, my.

This style would definitely take some getting used to. Perhaps it was the glasses that detracted from the overall appeal of the look, she thought charitably. Maybe if she only popped them on now and then during the evening, just to see where she was going, she would be okay. Reaching up, she lightly touched Sue Ellen's landscaping job and even though she'd never seen anything quite like it on the cover of *Metropolitan* magazine, she knew it was probably better than the bland way she used to wear her hair. Bravely, she decided to rely on Sue Ellen's expertise.

"Thank you, Sue Ellen," she breathed, squinting up at her friend through the dark glasses. "It's, uh, so creative."

Sue Ellen beamed. "I just know the guys will love it," she raved, clapping her hands excitedly. "Well, good luck learning all the little tricks of the trade tonight, honey. You couldn't have a better teacher. Why, I see Travis down at Little Joe's every once in a while on Friday nights, and I'm telling you, the women practically stand on their heads vying for his attention."

Wendy bristled. Nothing like learning from the best, she thought churlishly, then wondered at her sudden irritation with his popularity. After all, it was the main reason she was going out with him tonight. To learn to emulate his charisma. To learn the confidence and sex appeal that *Metropolitan* advised she would need to snare a man.

Sue Ellen began tossing her beauty tools into their respective suitcases. "Soon it'll be the same for you, honey." She snapped her cases shut and winked at Wendy. "From what I hear, the men are already lining up in droves down at the post office."

"I guess." Wendy shrugged bashfully. It was true. And if she was in the market for a geriatric husband, she'd be on cloud nine. But however ancient thirty might be according to the magazine article, she wasn't dead yet. She would hold out for a slightly younger man.

Grabbing her suitcases, Sue Ellen blew a couple of air kisses, wished her young friend the best, and was gone.

Wendy watched Sue Ellen drive away in a sea of dark green fuzz and sighed. Time to go strap her underwire bird cage to her chest and stuff her body into the minuscule purple cocktail dress that Beth had picked out for her.

Closing her front door, she slowly shook her head. She was beginning to think that other cultures had the right idea. Arranged marriages seemed infinitely more sensible than wasting all this precious time and energy trying to impress the opposite sex. Reaching up, she patted the stiff flower garden on her head. Darn. Sue Ellen had neglected to mention if she should water it or not.

"Travis!"

Travis could hear Faith calling him from the living room where she was resting with her feet up after having bathed Dusty and put him to bed.

"Yeah?" he asked distractedly. Why the hell couldn't he find his lucky bolo tie? Threading his hands through his hair, he stood in the middle of his bedroom and thought. It had to be around here somewhere.

"Wendy is here," Faith called.

"Tell her I'll be out in a minute," he called back. Damn. He hadn't even finished polishing his boots yet. Why had it taken him ten times longer to get ready for tonight's date than any other date he'd been on lately? And why the devil was he so worried about what Wendy thought about his appearance? He'd never cared what she thought of the way he looked before.

Must be the teacher thing, he thought by way of explanation to himself. He wanted to set a standard for her to observe. Show her the way it was done, so to speak. He wanted to prove to her that deep down inside, he had a gentlemanly streak.

Quickly pulling on his half-polished boots, he gave them a lick and a promise with an old rag. Listening with half an ear to the murmur of female voices coming from his living room, he popped a breath mint into his mouth, dabbed some after-shave on his jaw, checked his hair in the mirror and finally decided with a broad grin that, yes, he'd surely knock her dead. Lucky little thing. Getting an experienced guy like himself for her very own Henry Higgins.

Bounding down the hall to his living room, Travis reached the doorway and stopped dead in his tracks.

Good grief. What in tarnation had she done to her hair? It looked like something a racehorse would wear after winning the Kentucky Derby. He blinked rapidly to keep his eyes from popping out of his head. Slowly, he allowed them to travel south, and his jaw dropped.

"My stars..." he murmured as he stared at the scrappy, strappy, teeny-weeny purple cocktail dress that clung tenaciously to her nicely proportioned curves. He fought the sudden urge to rip off his jacket and throw it over her shoulders. She turned slowly to face him, wearing a funny, rather glazed look on her face.

"Hi, Travis." She smiled politely, looking just over his shoulder.

"Doesn't Wendy look nice, Travis?" Faith asked loyally. "Sue Ellen did her hair and makeup and Beth picked out the dress."

"Oh," Travis said, finally starting to come out of shock. That explained everything. Maybe he should tell her he liked it better when she did her own hair and makeup. He had a feeling ninety-nine percent of the male population of New Hope would agree with him. Then again, maybe it wouldn't be such a good idea to mess with her self-image at the moment. From the blank, almost unseeing look in her eyes, he could see she was feeling a little out of sorts.

"I feel kind of self-conscious," Wendy admitted, turning to stare wide-eyed just over Faith's shoulder. "Normally, this isn't the kind of thing I would choose to wear, but..." She sighed, a quirky smile tipping the corner of her mouth. "I'm trying to change my stodgy image. I know it needs work—" she grimaced and fingered a gladiola that drooped over her ear "—but for now, I'm leaning on the experts."

Her eyes shifted dully back to somewhere behind Travis, and he grinned at her, hoping to restore that sparkly, bright-eyed look she usually wore.

Faith nodded. "Sue Ellen is certainly an expert in the husband-hunting game." She moved over and slipped a supportive arm around Wendy's waist. "And I think with your darling figure, you are one of the very few women in New Hope that could successfully pull off this purple dress." She looked ruefully down at her own waist. "I'm beginning to wonder if I'll ever be able to wear something in my old size again."

"Sure you will," Wendy assured her. "And you'll have the added bonus of a wonderful bundle of joy to call your own. You're so lucky."

Travis watched a powerful look of yearning flash across Wendy's face and was surprised by the intensity he saw there. It was obvious that there was nothing she wanted more in the world than to get married and have a baby.

Once, a long time ago, he'd known that feeling. Babies really were a lot of fun. He'd never been able to understand how Elly Mae had been able to turn her back on her own baby. Especially one as wonderful as Dusty.

Well, he sighed, glancing at Wendy as she stood awkwardly in the middle of his living room looking like a scared rosebush caught in the headlights, he'd do everything in his power to help her accomplish her mission. She would make a wonderful mother. This he knew from the way she was with Dusty. She'd probably make a pretty darn good wife, too. She was a great listener. Criminy, she'd dragged the story about Elly Mae out of him without too much trouble, and he'd always hated to talk about that ancient history. Funny thing was, after he told her all about it, he'd been more at peace with that whole phase of his life than ever before.

And, knowing how ill at ease she felt at this very minute, he had to admire her courage. What she was doing took a lot of guts. Yeah, good ol' Wendy. She was just about as different from Elly Mae as anyone could possibly get. That must be one of the things he liked so much about her. He glanced at his watch. They'd better get a move on if they were going to make their reservation at Antonio's.

Hopefully, he thought, darting a glance at the flora and fauna on Wendy's head, Antonio would give them a table in the back. Way in the back.

After slipping the maître d' a healthy tip, Travis propelled Wendy after the small man as he led them to an intimate table for two in the farthest corner of the seldom used wing of the dark Italian restaurant. It would be worth the extra money to spare Wendy the humiliation of running into someone she knew with that weed patch on her head, Travis decided thoughtfully. Agnes would surely melt the phone lines over this one, he mused as he watched Wendy's delightful purple derriere weave its charming way through the restaurant. The maître d' gestured to their table, then headed back to his station.

Travis pushed her hands away from the back of her chair. "Would you knock it off?" he said under his breath. "You're supposed to give me a chance to help you into your seat."

"Sorry," she mumbled, her face growing pink as she stepped around to the front and then crouched and waited. Darn. She'd had a feeling she would forget this part. Lifting her behind slightly, she hovered in midair, while Travis positioned her chair for her. How silly, she thought, and re-adjusted the chair to a more comfortable spot after he'd finished. Why didn't the men just take care of their own chairs?

"Remind me to help you practice sitting down next time we have a lesson together," Travis said dryly as he took his own seat and tossed his red checkered napkin into his lap. "You don't have to lean over that way. Looks like you're trying to ski in a downhill race." Although he had to admit, with her firm little curves, she created a fetching picture. Probably would make a dandy little skier, too. Grinning, he leaned back in his chair and glanced around. Luckily they were completely alone. "And another thing. I'm supposed to handle your wrap. I'll help you in and out of it, okay? And when I open the car door for you, give me your hand. I'm supposed to help you up. Got that?"

"Well, for heaven's sake," she snapped, beginning to feel a little like her old self now that they had made it to the restaurant without mishap due to her nearsightedness. "I'm not an invalid." Unless he counted the fact that she couldn't see a blasted thing without her glasses.

"Well, if you want to learn the art of dating, you have to listen to me," he groused. "Personally, I couldn't care less if you want to bring your own chair and carry it in on your back. But then again, I'm liberated." His lips twitched with humor. "However, lots of guys don't like that in a woman. So, until you get used to the whole dating scene and find the guy that makes you comfortable, let's stick to the basics, okay?"

"Okay." She sighed and picked up her menu.

"New sunglasses?" Travis asked, puzzled as to why Wendy would be wearing dark glasses to study the menu in the already dark, romantic interior of Antonio's.

She glanced up and touched the ugly rims. "Uh, no. Actually, these belong to Sue Ellen. I borrowed them for tonight because as I was getting ready I washed my new contacts down the drain.''

Travis chuckled. Well, that would explain the death grip she'd had on his arm ever since they'd left his place. And the strange, blank look in her eyes. She couldn't see. As she removed the dark glasses and fumbled them into her purse, he leaned forward and studied her, knowing that she wouldn't be able to tell.

He had to admit, he liked her eyes the milk-chocolaty brown that they were now a lot better than the almost eerie, vivid blue contact lenses she'd been wearing. Her eyes were very lovely, really. Especially without her old glasses. Too bad she insisted on gluing those horrible false eyelashes to her lids. He liked her so much better in light makeup. Kind of like the way she looked the other day. During their dancing lesson. Reaching for his water glass, he took a swig as his mouth went suddenly dry.

Deciding to bite the bullet, Travis plunged into the subject of her new look. ''You know, Wendy,'' he began after the waiter had taken their order, ''you really don't need to wear quite so much goop on your face to attract a man's attention.'' *Aw, geez.* That didn't sound as diplomatic as he'd have liked. But it was too late to retract it now. Besides, it was true. If she ever wanted to catch a decent guy, she'd have to tone down the flashy accoutrements.

''But—'' Wendy's brows drew together in obvious puzzlement. ''I thought... I mean, *Metropolitan* magazine said—''

''Forget those stupid magazines for once, will you? You're letting them run your life.'' He leaned forward and studied her face in the candlelight. ''Besides, I think you have a very nice face, just the way it is. Hey, when you don't have your hair pulled back into that painful bun, and hide behind those disgusting glasses you used to wear, you're really kind of dishy.'' Grinning, he reached out and playfully squeezed her hand. She had such graceful, feminine, soft hands, he noted as something akin to an electrical current zapped him in the gut. Letting go of her hand, he picked up his fork and twiddled it absently.

"But," she argued plaintively, ignoring his compliments, "don't you think I need all this stuff to catch a man? I mean, I thought that's what you liked about BambiAnn."

Travis pulled his cheek between his teeth. She had a point there. He did like the buxom, blond, bimbo look on BambiAnn, and all of his other Saturday night specials that he'd yuck it up with down at Little Joe's Café. He just didn't like it on a nice girl like Wendy. For pity's sake, Wendy was the kind of girl you brought home to mother.

"Well . . ." he hedged, not wanting to sound like he had a double standard. "Makeup and sexy clothes are fine, but, you know, just not so much." To his mutual surprise and relief, Wendy looked glad.

"Oh, good," she sighed. "I know I couldn't have kept this routine up for too much longer. First of all, I'm not getting enough sleep. Do you know that it takes me two hours every morning to get my hair to stand on end the way Sue Ellen showed me?" With a sardonic glance down at her neckline, she brought her large, brown eyes up toward his. "Plus, the wires in my underwear are killing me."

Me, too, Travis wanted to say, daring a quick peek at the lush hills of her creamy white cleavage. He was tempted to tell her to keep the underwire underwear and the low-cut, peek a boo blouses. But something deep inside didn't like the idea of her future boyfriends getting a load of this view.

"Trust me," he said instead. "You don't need all this stuff to catch a man. Just be yourself. It will happen."

"Travis," she sighed, propping her chin on her elbow and rolling her eyes, "I've been just myself for nearly thirty years now, and look where it has gotten me. I'm still as single and inexperienced as the day I was born."

"So what?" Travis asked, finding the fact that she hadn't been out with a lot of men refreshing. Somewhat titillating, even. "I'm not married, either. Lots of people our age and older aren't married and live very happy and productive lives."

"True," she murmured slowly as she thought about his words.

"You should count your blessings." Holding up his hand, he began to count them on his fingers for her. "You have a wonderful job that you really seem to like. You have the respect and friendship of almost everyone in the town of New Hope. You live in a great house and have super neighbors." He chuckled. "What more could you want?"

"A little boy, like Dusty," she said softly, lifting her liquid gaze to his.

His heart skipped a beat. "In a way," he said, his voice as low as hers, "you do. He loves you like a mother."

The candlelight from the small dancing flame on the table sparkled in Wendy's eyes as she beamed up at him. "I feel the same way about him." Her smile was beguiling.

"He knows," Travis assured her, and reached out to take her hand in his. Might as well teach her how to hold hands, he reasoned. The way her skin looked so smooth and soft and milky and . . . kissable there in the dim glow of the restaurant, he could almost begin to understand his son's fascination with the girl next door.

Later that evening—after a fantastic meal at the terminally romantic Antonio's, where Travis had discovered that talking to an intelligent woman could be a turn-on—they slowly climbed the stairs to her front porch. Reaching the top, they stopped and turned toward each other. Travis clenched and unclenched his fists, feeling suddenly nervous and awkward. Not since he'd shared his first kiss with Elly Mae had he felt quite so...so...excited. What the devil was the matter with him? It wasn't as if he was the novice here.

"I'm sorry, I forgot to leave the porch light on," Wendy apologized as she felt around the inside of her purse for her house keys.

"That's okay," Travis said, lifting the gargantuan purse from her arms and plopping it on the porch floor. "For this part of the lesson, moonlight will work just fine."

"What part?" Wendy asked, pursing her lips in consternation.

"The good-night-kiss part," he explained patiently. If she was going to date, she'd have to learn to handle the good-night kiss. Better from him than from some stranger. And he had a feeling from comments she'd made throughout the week that she was woefully inexperienced when it came to this particular art. Lucky for her, he'd had lots of practice in the area, he thought smugly. For some juvenile reason he was looking forward to giving the straitlaced postmistress the thrill of her life. Showing the wallflower how the big boys played ball. When he was done with her lips, she wouldn't know her own name.

"The, uh, good-night-kiss part?" she squeaked, and cleared her throat. "Is a good-night kiss usually part of the first date?"

"Wendy..." He sighed in exasperation. Usually, he didn't have to convince his dates that they needed a kiss. "This is the nineties, okay? A good-night kiss will be the least of your worries." He'd teach her some karate moves later in the week, to fend off unwanted advances, he decided as the unpleasant image of some Lothario or another groping Wendy flickered through his mind.

She heaved a huge, resigned sigh. "Okay. You're right. Let's do it." Angling her face up to him, she waited patiently for him to begin.

Well, dammit, she didn't have to sound so enthused, he thought disgruntledly. "Okay, but if I'm going to take you seriously, we're going to have to lose these distracting eyelashes and some of the horticulture on your head." Reaching up, he began to weed out the ostentatiousness.

"Ow," she complained, peeling away the eyelashes and batting at his helpful hands. "Here, wait," Wendy instructed. "Let me help."

Slowly, as Travis watched beneath the soft glow of the moon, she lifted her arms and began to pull the plethora of pins from her hair. As though she were performing a sexy striptease, he felt his eyes begin to glaze over. The flowers fell out of her sun-streaked, loosely curled tresses and landed at their feet in a heap of petals. Then, one by one, the pins followed, until, with a shake of her glorious head, her wild, wonderful golden hair was flowing in unfettered waves down her back.

Wow, Travis thought, dampening his lips with the tip of his tongue. *That was a lot better.* Now, perhaps, he could continue with his lesson. He coughed slightly, to clear some nebulous obstruction in his throat.

"Okay," he began masterfully, in a valiant effort to regain the upper hand. "Uh, first of all, I—or, of course, whoever he will be—will say something like this. 'Uh, Wendy, I had a great time tonight. We'll have to do it again real soon and, uh, blah-blah-blah' like that, and you will respond with this— Repeat after me now—" He tilted her chin and looked deeply into her eyes. "Oh, Travis, I had a wonderful time tonight, blah-blah-blah . . .''

He could tell she wasn't concentrating. "Come on, Wendy," he said sternly. "You have to concentrate. Now, go ahead, repeat after me."

Wendy snorted. "I feel utterly ridiculous standing here, saying these absurd things to you. You're my neighbor, for heaven's sake, Travis. It's hard for me to emote this way."

"Who said anything about emoting? Just repeat after me."

"Oh, Travis," she deadpanned. "I had a wonderful time tonight, blah-blah-blah."

"Very funny. Okay. Now, then. I'll take you in my arms, like...uh—" he reached around her waist and pulled her up against his chest "—this, and then...you put your arms up around my neck, like so."

"Is this really necessary?" Wendy sighed. "It seems like such a waste of time."

"Just do it," he retorted crabbily. "Then, you look adoringly up at me."

"I can't even see you without my glasses," she complained.

"Fake it," he snapped.

For the love of Mike, Travis thought, beginning to lose his patience. Kissing a rattlesnake would be easier than kissing this obstinate woman. No wonder she didn't have much experience in the art of the good-night kiss. She probably scared the few dates she'd managed to snag half to death with her overanalysis. Lucky for her, she'd met her match.

Wendy shot him her best look of adoration.

"Good. And then I look down at you like this," he said, and demonstrated how her future boyfriend would probably cradle her cheeks in his palms. "That's how you know the man is going to kiss you," he told her, his lips hovering slightly above hers as he spoke. He could feel her breath, whisper-soft as it fanned his face. She had the sweetest breath. And she smelled so good. She was trembling, he thought hazily as he went in for the kill. What a turn-on. He couldn't remember the last time he'd caused a woman to tremble. He fought the slight tremor in his own legs.

Slowly, slowly, ever so slowly, Travis lowered his lips to hers. And, all the while, he knew that he was going to be giving innocent little Wendy the thrill of her life.

What Travis didn't count on the moment his lips found hers—ready, pliant and open—was the feeling that he'd been yanked off the front porch by a Texas tornado, electrocuted, punched in the gut, spun around and set back down with his boots on the wrong feet.

What the Sam Hill had just happened here? he wondered, dazed by the mind-bending impact of her kiss.

Then again, who cared?

Plunging his hands into her wild tresses, he yanked her mouth back up to his and went back for seconds.

6

As Travis continued his assault on her senses, Wendy began to fear she would soon need the assistance of a paramedic. Thready pulse, weak knees, a roaring in her ears, surely these were the symptoms of something fatal happening to her body. Never before, in all of her twenty-nine-plus years, had she ever experienced anything so...so...thrilling. And scary. And wonderful.

His mouth was so warm and soft, yet at the same time, demanding. And as those sweet, sensuous lips moved over hers, coaxing her to respond, to open, to submit to him, something changed in Wendy. With his kiss, he was teaching her things about herself she'd never known and would never—for the rest of her life—forget.

She was a passionate person, she was suddenly discovering as she greedily threaded her hungry hands into Travis's thick hair and pulled him even closer than he already was. Lips moved, mouths tasted, lungs labored, and small, intense moans of pleasure filled both throats. It was all becoming so crystal clear, she thought joyfully, tossing her curly, honey-streaked mane of hair over her shoulders and wriggling in closer against Travis as he plundered her eager mouth.

Now it all made sense. Had she but known what thrills lay within a man's embrace, perhaps she would have risked her parents' censure, the way her sister Wanda had. No wonder

Wanda had climbed out the window to meet her boyfriends after lights-out each night. No wonder BambiAnn made such a glamour girl production out of catching herself a man. It was all worth it, if this was her payoff each Friday night. The girl wasn't as dumb as she put on, Wendy thought admiringly.

Now that she knew the secret magic of a real good-night kiss, she'd give old BambiAnn a run for her money in the ingenue department. She'd prove that she could catch herself a man with the best of them. Heck, she'd scale Mt. Everest in her torturous high heels and underwire bra, if it meant getting another one of these mind-boggling kisses from Travis.

Mmm, she thought as Travis pulled her lower lip into his mouth and between his teeth. Yes, she would happily glue those silly false eyelashes to her eyes, and stick fresh flowers in her hair at the crack of dawn every morning, if it meant spending another moment in his arms. She'd speak with the florist tomorrow about setting up an account, she decided hazily.

Then again, a niggling thought worried her as she struggled for what was left of her rational mind. *Travis?* Surely she couldn't be serious. Gracious sakes, she couldn't allow herself to go and get a puppy-dog crush on the first man to really kiss her, now could she? No. Experimentally, Wendy ran the tip of her tongue over his lower lip as she tried to organize her thoughts. But, it was hard. To organize her thoughts, that is, with him kissing her that way.

Travis was not the man of her dreams, no matter how he might excite her physically. Heavens, no. He was far too much of a wild man to ever take seriously as husband material. And before she got too addicted to his firm lips, his hard body, his thick hair, and his considerable prowess in the lovemaking department, perhaps she should shop around.

Yes. That was a good idea. Maybe she would experience this intoxicating rush with another man. A man who would make a good father to her children. A man who she could talk to. Have fun with. A man who could make her toes curl the way they were curling now. It was obvious she was going to have to do some research on this matter. Purely academic, of course. After all, Travis couldn't be the only single man on the face of the earth capable of turning her knees to quicksand.

A low, male, primal groan of satisfaction filled her ears as Travis swept great handfuls of her hair into his fists and tugged her head to the side so that he could demonstrate his rather extensive talents on her neck. Gasping, Wendy clung to his forearms for support. Had she known how enjoyable these lessons could be, she'd have asked for his help ages ago. She slid her hands from his arms to his broad chest and, clutching his shirt tightly between her fingers, dragged his mouth back to hers.

It was warm for the late October evening and the harvest moon hung low in the sky, illuminating them as they stood entwined in the shadows of Wendy's front porch. Somewhere, the night song of some pond frogs sounded gently in the background, but otherwise, with the exception of their ragged breathing, all was quiet.

Disquieting thoughts surged through Travis's subconscious. He just could not believe what was happening. Lord have mercy, he'd kissed plenty of women in his time, all kinds, all ages, all shapes and sizes, but never, ever—not even under the Jackrabbit bleachers the first time with Elly Mae—had he ever felt like this. It was almost as if he wore some kind of virtual reality headset and had stepped onto another planet. The planet of Technicolor passion.

Why hadn't he ever noticed the tigress that lurked beneath the horn-rims before? Usually his radar could detect that stuff a mile off. Must be what made her so fascinating, he guessed as he dove into her kiss and proceeded to drown in her arms. Her looks were deceiving. She was an enigma. This woman should come with a warning label. Caution: Objects Are Hotter Than They Appear. Continued Exposure May Be Hazardous To Your Health.

"Ah," Wendy sighed, allowing her head to drop back on her shoulders as she leaned against the firm circle of his arms. "So," she murmured huskily as he continued to feast upon the soft hollow of her throat, "how'd I do?"

Still on the alternate passion planet, Travis dipped his tongue into the delicate curve of her collarbone and tasted her staccato pulse. "How'd you do what?" he asked, his mind a fuzzy wad of cotton candy.

Her quick intake of breath pleased him.

"You know..." she groaned slowly as her eyes fell closed and her head lolled back against his shoulder. Taking a steadying breath, she peered up at him through the thick fringe of her own naturally heavy lashes. "Are my kisses...you know, uh..." She sighed. "Date worthy?"

Date worthy? Was she *kidding?* Hers were the lips that battles were fought over. She could conquer nations with these lips. Launch ships. Bring sane, rational men to their knees.

And the most beautiful thing of all was—she had no idea.

Suddenly, Travis couldn't stand the thought of her taking her kisses anywhere else. Dammit anyway. He'd found them. They were his. As much as he wanted to reassure her, to build her confidence, to tell her how much she'd affected him—*him*, the man who hadn't felt anything for a woman since his heart had shattered into a billion slivers over three years ago—he couldn't bring himself to do it. She just wasn't ready for the harsh realities of the dating world. It was up to him to protect her. And teach her.

"Well..." He sighed, raking a frustrated and somewhat guilty hand through his hair. Frustrated, because he wanted to take her innocence for his own, but knew he couldn't, and guilty because of what he intended to tell her.

"Well?" she asked, tentatively peeking through the darkness to his face.

He crossed his fingers behind her back. "Well, uh, I'd say you could use a little work. Nothing major, just a little fine-tuning here and there. I'd, uh . . ." Pausing, he cleared his throat. "Be happy to have another practice session with you, you know . . . uh, say, tomorrow? After Dusty is in bed?" He tried valiantly to keep the note of desperation from his voice as he released her from his embrace. He had to move away from her. It was that, or explode.

Wendy's sigh was dejected. "I'm sorry, Travis. I know you're used to much more experienced, worldly, beautiful women, and I feel bad about having to put you through this whole ordeal again. I just feel so sorry that it couldn't have been more pleasant for you." Crushed, she hung her head.

Any more pleasant, and he'd be dead, he thought, feeling like a first-class heel. She looked so abashed, standing there, holding her insecurities up for his inspection. It was all he could do not to drag her back into his arms and whisper the truth to her. That she was a hell of a woman, and he wanted to take her to new and even more exciting heights of passion.

But she wasn't ready yet. Wendy was a nice girl. The marrying kind. He couldn't turn an innocent babe in the woods like her over to a bunch of wolves like the ones she had written on her list. No. He had her best interests in mind. He would gently help her take her first tentative steps toward womanhood. After all, it was the least he could do for the person his son considered a second mother. Hell, she was practically family. He was obligated.

Reaching up, he pulled a strand of honey-streaked hair away from her soft pink lips. Did she have any clue how perfect she looked just now? Most likely not.

"I don't want to take advantage of your help," she was still explaining, protesting his offer. "I know you have a full social calendar."

"Oh, hey," he hastened to reassure her. "Nothing that can't wait. Listen, if we're going to beat your deadline on this dating game of yours, we should practice hard and heavy for several weeks and then, uh..." Realizing what he'd just suggested, he faltered, then surged ahead to cover. "And you know, get you ready for bachelor number one. My social life will be there waiting for me when we're finished."

Unfortunately, he lamented to himself. Truth be told, he was dying for an excuse to cool it with the hostage-taking BambiAnn. He just hadn't had the motivation. Until now. Now, he needed to keep an eye on Wendy.

"Okay. If you're sure." She sighed, the heavy burden of her inexperience written all over her face. "Well, I don't want to keep you. It's getting late, and I know Faith is probably anxious to get home, so I guess I'll see you in the morning."

Travis lifted her purse off the porch and handed it to her. He stood waiting as she searched for and finally located her keys. "Yes," he agreed, strangely eager to see her again, as soon as possible. Even if it was during the morning rush hour. Man. He was really getting into this teacher act. Maybe he should chill. It wouldn't be too smart to go and get overly involved with her personal life. It's just that no one had ever looked to him for this kind of advice before. It was heady stuff. He'd have to be careful how he handled her.

"Okay, then." She smiled tiredly as her bolt lock slid back and she was able to push her door open. "I'll see you in the morning."

"Okay," he agreed, waxing poetic in his head about yonder light as he tried to bring his breathing under control. Mercy, mercy, mercy. That was it. He needed to have his head examined. "Good night," he whispered, wishing she would turn so that he could kiss her one last time.

"Good night," she returned, before slipping through the door and gently clicking it shut.

After having completed Phases I through V of Sue Ellen's facial cleansing ritual, Wendy slipped into the skimpy baby dolls that Beth had chosen for her and climbed into bed. There, she stared vacantly out the window at the large, golden harvest moon and thought about what had just happened with Travis on her front porch.

A part of her wanted to pretend that Travis was her true love and that the electric ardor she thought she felt radiating from him was real. A part of her wanted to revel in the sheer ecstasy of the moment. The same part that wanted to believe he was lying in his own bed right now—his head still spinning from the effects of their shared passion—as frustrated as she was.

But, she knew that was not true.

No. Wendy was sure that as far as Travis was concerned, what had happened was simply another day at the office. Most likely, he could have phoned in his part, as well rehearsed as he obviously was. And the performances he'd just given her, on the porch that acted as the stage to her dating lessons, spoke of years of practice.

Gracious. What would have happened if he'd actually been turned on out there? Chances were she wouldn't be alive right now to tell the tale. Because any more sizzle from his camp and she'd have gone up in flames. Did all women react to him that way? she wondered, and yawned. Did BambiAnn?

Even more important was the question of how she would react to another man's kiss . . . another man's touch . . . his caress. Would any man set her on fire the way Dusty's dad did?

Well, she decided sleepily as she plumped her pillow, more aware now than ever before of the empty, hollow ache in her heart. If she wanted answers to that one, she was going to have to glean as much knowledge from Travis as she could, then test it out on bachelor number one. Yawning broadly again, she curled onto her side and wondered if Travis was regretting his decision to teach her how to date. She hoped she hadn't been too much of a drag tonight. She knew how he liked his women.

Too bad, she thought muzzily as her eyes drifted shut. Too bad that she and Travis were so...incompatible. Because...she mused, her sleep-heavy thoughts muddled and incoherent, in many ways...they...were...so perfect for...each other.

Saturday morning finally arrived, bringing with it Halloween and a long list of chores for Travis to accomplish before the festivities began that evening. Pushing the button on his dashboard that activated his garage door opener, Travis—carefully avoiding Dusty's bicycle—pulled into his garage. He cut the engine, hopped out of the cab and released the latch to the canopy that covered the trucks bed. Inside the dark cubby lay enough groceries to last at least a month. Travis grinned to himself as he loaded his arms. Although, the way Dusty was packing it away these days, he'd probably be back at the grocery store by the end of the week.

Happy squeals greeted him as he nudged the kitchen door open and set his packages on the drainboard.

"Booooo!" Dusty's cry rang from the living room as he clumped clumsily around under the infernal sheet he'd been wearing all week.

"Oh, no!" Wendy protested in mock terror. "Please don't scare me, Mr. Ghost!" Travis could hear her running across the living room, Dusty flapping along after her.

"I won't scare ya, you old sidewinder! But, I'll wrastle ya!" More thumping, squeals and giggling followed as Dusty hurled himself at Wendy and dragged her to the ground, where he proceeded to gambol on her, over her and around her, puppy fashion.

Smiling, Travis headed to the garage and collected the last of his groceries. There was nothing like a five-year-old's gleeful laughter. And no one could make Dusty laugh the way Wendy could.

Wendy. It had been two long days since he kissed her on the porch after their first lesson. In those two days, Travis figured maybe one—two at the most—of his wakeful hours had been spent *not* thinking about Wendy. What in tarnation was wrong with him? He never spent this much time dwelling on a woman. But, dammit anyway. If that kiss wasn't enough to give him brain damage, then her cockamamy scheme to catch a man was.

Unfortunately, Dusty had come down with an earache while they were out Wednesday night, and Travis had been unable to help her with any more lessons that week. Just as well. He'd made a decision. No more kissing practice. No way.

He'd wasted enough time daydreaming about that. It wasn't healthy, all this fantasizing about his neighbor, the postmistress. Envisioning her in skimpy swimsuits and lacy underthings. For crying in the night. She was the paragon of New Hope virtue. Why did he suddenly find that concept so...titillating? That must be what everyone, including himself, found so fascinating about her these days. That virginal vamp thing she had going there.

Criminy, he thought, disgruntled as he began to put the refrigerated items away. The line of leering, wolfish old men down at the post office was growing by leaps and bounds. For the past two days it had been all he could do to keep from marching behind the counter and buying a year's supply of one-cent stamps for old Ralph and the boys. Anything to get rid of her geriatric fan club.

It seemed to him that since she'd taken his advice and toned down the wild hair, gotten some new, clear contact lenses, and stopped troweling the makeup on quite so heavily, she was getting more attention than ever. Perhaps he should tell her to go back to the garish garden look, he thought possessively. The way everyone was fawning over her made him want to gag.

And what scared him more than anything was the fact that her plan seemed to be working. She had men coming out her ears. None of them was worth a plug nickel in the husband category, but it irked him just the same. Although *why* it irked him remained a mystery.

Must be because of Dusty. If Wendy went off and got married and had a bunch of kids, what would happen to Dusty? Would she forget him? Travis didn't think so. Not intentionally, anyway, but just the same, the thought was unsettling. Plus, who would he rely on, when he needed to go somewhere? When he needed someone to bounce an idea off? When he needed someone to talk to? Laugh with? Tease, and be teased by? He was only just beginning to understand how much he counted on Wendy for those things since Elly Mae left. Why hadn't he been able to see that before?

Because her shoes had been in the way. And, her bottle-bottom glasses.

He snorted and shook his head. Since Elly Mae left, he'd spent far too much time in shallow water. Well, he sighed, folding the multitude of brown paper bags that had held his groceries, one good thing had come from Wendy's goofy plan. It had woken him up. Time to join the real world again. His self-destructive, wild-man life-style had been one way to get through the rough spots, but it was time to rejoin the human race. Time to start acting his age again. Time to think about the future. His and Dusty's.

"Dad! You're home!" Dusty charged into the kitchen and leapt up into Travis's arms. "Did you remember to get some candy? It's Tricken Treaten tonight, ya know," he reminded him excitedly.

How could he forget? "Yep," he said, and lifted his Stetson off his head to plop it on Dusty's as he set his son back down on the floor. "I got enough to give every kid in New Hope at least one cavity." Lifting his eyes, they collided with Wendy's as she entered the room.

Her cheeks were flushed from her wrestling match with the young boy, her curly blond hair was bound loosely in a wild, flyaway ponytail, and she was wearing those blasted skintight jeans and a formfitting, light blue sweater. Aw, man. Just what he was afraid of. She was a damn vision. His gut clenched and he licked his dry lips.

"Hi," she said shyly, averting her gaze.

"Hi," he returned, puzzled by his own bashfulness. Ever since the big kiss, they'd been as awkward around each other as two football players in ballet class. This was also different for Travis. Made him feel about twenty years younger than he was. Although, he had to admit, the feeling was not altogether unpleasant.

"Dad, I asked Wendy to go Tricken Treaten with us tonight, 'kay?" Dusty's eyes fairly danced at the thought.

Travis's gaze slowly traveled from his son back to Wendy. "Well, now, if she's going to do something so... exciting, we want it to be with us, right, Dusty?"

"Yeah!" Dusty jumped for joy.

The double entendre was not lost on Wendy. The devilish twinkle in Travis's eyes had her heart ricocheting off her ribs as she was suddenly transported to the circle of his arms and Wednesday night's good-night kiss. And though the memories had her stomach in an uncomfortable twist, it was wonderful to have Travis teasing her again. For the past two days he'd seemed vaguely distant—nearly put off—and she couldn't help but wonder if it was because she'd been so hopeless as a dating partner.

"So—" Travis leaned comfortably back against his dishwasher and crossed his legs at the ankles "—can you join us tonight? Dusty's earache is a lot better, although, I think if he were on his death bed, I couldn't keep him down tonight." Absently, he reached out and ruffled his son's silky blond locks. "It's all he's been talking about for weeks now."

Turning, Wendy smiled fondly at the child. "You're sure you feel up to it?" she asked, motherly concern tingeing her voice.

"'Course! I'm all better. Right, Dad?" He looked worriedly back and forth between the two adults, as if he feared they may keep him home. "Come on, Wendy. You hafta come Tricken Treaten with us tonight." Dusty trained his large pleading gaze up at her. "Please? I'll give you some of my candy."

Giving her head a slight shake, Wendy laughed. "How can I resist such an enticing offer?" Her glance darted to Travis, then shot quickly back to Dusty. "That is, if it's okay with your dad."

Travis folded his arms across his broad chest and lifted his shoulders slightly. "Fine by me. In fact, it would probably be a good chance for you to practice some of your dating skills," he said, his voice nonchalant. He waved a casual hand. "I owe you another one for taking care of Dusty this morning. So, we could kill two birds with one stone, if you want."

Wendy deliberated for a moment. She knew she needed all the help she could get on the dating front. And having Dusty along would forestall another one of those mind-boggling kissing lessons. Which was good, since she'd made a decision not to kiss Travis anymore. It might not have affected him in the least, but she hadn't been able to concentrate at work for two days now. If she was going to get this hung up over one little kiss, she wanted it to be with a guy she could consider marrying. Looking down at Dusty, she saw him looking hopefully up at her.

"Okay. How about if I meet you guys here just before it starts getting dark? I can help you with your costume that way, Dusty."

"Goodie!" Dusty beamed up at his dad.

"Sounds great," Travis agreed, perturbed to discover that he was nearly as excited as his son about the prospect of spending the evening with Wendy.

"'Bye, Mrs. Deane," Travis called to their elderly neighbor, who'd agreed to pass out candy at the Donovan house while they took Dusty out that evening. "And thanks."

"Come on, Wendy! C'mon, Dad!" Dusty was already flying down the front walkway, his plastic jack-o'-lantern thumping hollowly against his legs as he went. Dusk had settled over the cozy cul-de-sac and, one by one, the stars were beginning to appear. Little ghosts and goblins darted hither and yon, gathering candy and compliments.

"Dusty," Wendy called, looking up at Travis helplessly. "Watch where you're going, will you? And stay out of the street."

"Okay," he called, charging up the front steps to the Deane home. "Tricken Treat!" he shouted at the top of his lungs when Mr. Deane opened the door and feigned heart-stopping fear at the apparition that stood belt level on his front porch.

"Oh, my! What have we here?" the old man asked with a craggy smile.

"I'm Casper!" Dusty hollered. "Boo!"

Travis gripped Wendy's arm and, pulling her close, whispered in her ear, "You've got him convinced that he's pretty scary." He grinned indulgently in Casper's direction.

When Travis didn't immediately let go of her arm, Wendy guessed that he must be starting the dating lessons again, and tried to relax. Tried to pretend that this was not the man who'd opened the Pandora's box of her dormant sensual life, but instead a comfortable old friend, on whom she could practice her social skills. As she leaned toward him, she felt his arm travel naturally around her shoulders, where it lay in a loose, brotherly hold.

"Did you say thank you?" Travis asked as Dusty tripped down the stairs and ran to where they stood waiting on the sidewalk.

"Thank you!" Dusty cried over his shoulder before galloping into the next yard.

Wendy felt a smile start in her stomach and spread to her cheeks. Travis, for all his faults, was a really terrific father. She'd consider herself to be very lucky if her future husband was even half the father Travis Donovan was. And come to think of it, she mused as Travis led her down the street after their half-pint ghost, aside from his penchant for dating half the town of New Hope, he didn't really have that many faults. He was a wonderful father, a hard worker, a solid citizen, and a kick to spend the evening just watching TV with. Or arguing with. Or teasing. He was a pretty good friend to her, actually. Funny how she'd never really noticed how much she'd come to depend on his steady presence right next door these past three years.

"So," Travis began easily as they strolled after Dusty. "What else can I teach you about dating?"

Her entire body flushed at the possibilities. "Um, well, uh, let's see," she stammered, suddenly tongue-tied. How unusual. She never felt this awkward around Travis. Perhaps it was because he had pulled her hand into his at her shoulder and laced their fingers together. Or perhaps it was the way he was absently rubbing the pad of his thumb over her knuckles. "Well, let me think here." She shot him a sideways glance. "Probably, it would be easier for me to tell you what I do know about dating. It would take a lot less time."

She could feel his chuckle resonate from where his chest touched her shoulder. "Okay, I get the picture," he said.

Wendy was relieved to note that he didn't seem put off, or disgusted by her lack of experience. In fact, if she didn't know better, she'd think he was pleased. Probably saw her as a challenge, she thought, feeling a little bit like second prize in a charity raffle.

"How about if we just practice holding hands and walking like this for a while?" he suggested. "Get you used to some hand-holding and such, while we make light conversation." Imperceptibly, his grip on her fingers tightened as he squeezed her shoulders.

"Okay," she mumbled, missing a step and gripping his waist with her free hand.

"Careful," he admonished, his voice low and sexy in her ear as he caught her and locked her arm at his waist. "So, I take it that someday, you want to have a few little ghosts and goblins of your own?" Travis threw a line into the conversational pond. "Is that the reason for the big rush to become engaged before you turn thirty?"

"Mmm." Wendy nodded as they stopped in front of yet another house while Dustin did his best to terrify the owners. "That's a big part of it. I'd like to have several children, and if I'm going to do that, I'd better get a move on. I don't want to be chasing them around with my walker," she giggled.

"Oh, you're pretty ancient," he said mockingly.

"Easy for you to say. You already have the best little boy in Texas."

"True."

"I'd trade everything I have for a little one just like him," she said wistfully, and nodded at Casper as he stumbled down his latest conquest's front steps toward them.

Travis pulled her close and planted a tender kiss at her temple. "I meant it the other night when I told you that he feels the same way about you."

Embarrassed, Wendy's gaze flitted to his. "I know."

They stood for a moment, looking into each other's eyes, until Dusty crowded between them. "Look! Popcorn balls from Mrs. Peterson!" Unable to contain his joy, Dusty took off in a vapor of ghostly glee and headed for the next porch.

Taking a healthy step back from Wendy, Travis ran his hand over his mouth. Manachevits. He had to get a grip on his thoughts when it came to Wendy these days. For a minute there, he could almost picture her as a stepmother to his son. Lightly, he rubbed his five o'clock shadow. He'd gone and gotten too involved. Just like he warned himself not to. Time to cut her loose. To let her try her wings. Okay, so she probably wasn't ready to solo yet, but it would probably be good for both of them if she got herself interested in another man. Quick.

"You know," he began offhandedly, "I think you might be ready to pick a guy on your list for a date."

"Really?" Wendy stopped walking and peered up at him through the gloaming.

"Mmm-hmm." He nodded, watching Dusty stand on tiptoe to reach an out-of-the-way doorbell. It was a good idea. So, why did he hate it so much?

"Okay," she said uncertainly. "If you think I'm ready, I'll give Cecil Yates a call tomorrow and ask him out."

Yech. Travis grimaced inwardly. *Cecil Yates?* "Okay, fine. I'll call BambiAnn, and we'll double."

"Double?"

"Uh, yeah," he hedged. "You may need me nearby to, uh, you know, coach you, or something."

Wendy smiled gratefully up at him. "Good idea."

"Great," he said, nodding in approval. "Maybe we could even invent some code words or signals or something, in case you're doing something wrong."

"Okay."

Good. It was a good idea. He liked having a little control over the proceedings. For Wendy's sake, of course. "We'll work on that tomorrow afternoon, and by then, maybe we'll have our dates nailed down." Reaching out, he took her hand in his. At her questioning glance he said, "Just some last-minute warm-up exercises."

7

The following day found Wendy and Travis in his back-yard, enjoying the lazy, crystal-clear Sunday afternoon as they lounged on his deck chairs, drinking ice tea. Wendy had brought with her a pad of paper and a pen to take notes regarding Wednesday night's double date with Cecil Yates and BambiAnn Howe. Dusty sat contentedly at their feet, sorting through the mountain of candy and goodies he'd collected the evening before and reveling in time spent with his two favorite people in the world.

Cecil had been surprised and flattered by Wendy's phone invitation to join her and Travis and BambiAnn for dinner down at Little Joe's Café on Wednesday night. The slight, balding man had jumped at the suggestion, telling her that he'd been meaning to ask her out for a long time now. His eager acceptance gave Wendy courage, and now she felt reasonably sure—with the help of some last-minute coaching from Travis—that she was finally on the road to achieving her goal.

Cecil, although he was no Travis Donovan in the looks department, seemed like a pleasant enough fellow. Mild mannered, hugely intelligent, and most important, single. A self-made millionaire in the super-computing industry, Cecil reminded Wendy somewhat of herself when it came to his social life. He was a bit of a loner, concentrating on his career, and Wendy suspected he'd never had much experience dating.

And though Cecil was easy enough to talk to on a business basis down at the post office—gracious, he could talk all day about the inner workings of a computer—Wendy had to admit she was grateful that Travis and BambiAnn would be there to take the conversational pressure off.

Now, if she could just get these crazy, secret signals that Travis insisted on, down pat, she'd be ready. Unfortunately, they only had a few days to practice, and Travis seemed to think that she wouldn't be able to find her fork without a cue from him.

"Okay," Travis continued, taking a thoughtful sip of his ice tea. "When I scratch my jaw, that means you should remember to let Cecil help you with your chair, or your wrap."

"Oh, brother," she muttered, shaking her head. A slight furrow of concentration marred Wendy's brow as she jotted down his instructions. "Okay, jaw scratch equals 'remember to let Cecil help.' Um—" her eyes scanned her pad "—what does pulling on your ear mean again?"

"Ask him a question about himself. Draw him out. People love that." Nodding, he gestured to her notes. "Read back what we have so far."

She flipped back to the front page. "Uh, okay. If you shrug your shoulders, I should ask Cecil to dance. If you pinch the bridge of your nose, I should move a little closer to Cecil. If you cough, I can graduate to blowing in his ear..." She glanced up at Travis. "I don't know about that one, Travis. It seems a little forward."

The slight shake of his head was vaguely amused. "Would you trust me on this? Listen. Today is November first. You only have a month left, before you turn thirty. If you're going to succeed in being engaged by then, you're going to have to get aggressive, especially when it comes to a little weasel like Cecil Yates. Criminy, Wendy, *he'll* never get around to making the first move," Travis huffed knowingly. "If I leave it up to the two of you, you'll never get anywhere."

Wendy shot him a beleaguered glare. "He's not a weasel."

His dimples deepened as he curled his upper lip and rolled his eyes up at the clear, autumn sky. "Whatever. And since you're not overly pushy by nature, you're going to need my help on Wednesday night. Trust me. Some light coaching will help you relax and sail through the evening. You'll be really glad we did this."

"I don't know," she sighed. "Most of these things are so foreign to me . . . blowing in his ears and whatnot. Plus . . ." She peeked woefully at him from under her lashes. "I know I'm not very good at the physical stuff yet." A gentle breeze tugged at the pages of her notes and she smoothed them down with her hand.

Yet? Travis mulled over the word in his mind, his eyes following the simple gesture of her fingertips lightly skimming the dancing paper. Oh, have mercy, what would it be like to kiss Wendy when she finally felt competent at what she called "the physical stuff"? His gut tightened and burned and he knew he couldn't think about that. It wasn't good for his blood pressure.

Swallowing, he shifted uncomfortably in his chair. It was a good thing the harmless Cecil Yates would be her first real date. Travis didn't think he could stand the thought of her getting even a tiny bit physical with another man. Since Cecil fell somewhat short in the manly category, he guessed he could tolerate the idea of a good-night kiss between the two of them. Barely.

"Uh, you shouldn't worry about having to make all the moves," he informed her, a slight edge to his voice.

"Oh?" she asked, glad that she could count on Cecil to pick up the slack. As Travis scowled at his shoes for a moment, Wendy knew he was probably thinking that after one of her bungled attempts at a good-night kiss, poor Cecil would never call again. Taking a deep breath, she let it out slowly and hoped that Cecil's inexperience would be her ally. Hopefully, he wouldn't know a good kiss from a bad one, the way Travis did.

Taking a healthy gulp of his ice tea, Travis glanced up at her. "I guess you should just watch me and BambiAnn. Besides, once you give old Cecil the idea that you are interested, he'll probably take the initiative." He jangled the cubes in his glass. "What else have you got?"

"Well . . ." She looked dubiously down at her pad. "There's the one where you smile and nod, and I'm supposed to remember to laugh gaily. And the one where you wink, and I'm supposed to reach out and do something familiar, like straighten his collar or hair." She sent a sidelong glance into the light gray pool of Travis's eyes. He really did have beautiful eyes. Much nicer than Cecil's small, rather dull, brown ones. "Travis, are you sure about this? Why can't I just treat Cecil like I always do? Wouldn't that work?"

Travis blew an arrogant puff of air. "No."

"But why not? This secret signal routine just seems so complicated. Not to mention . . . devious."

Several birds twittered innocently from a tree overhead, lending to Wendy's feelings of doubt. Poor Cecil. He was free as a birdie now. What would he make of her plans to capture him in the web of domestic tranquillity she was spinning?

"Oh, get over it," Travis advised, leaning forward, elbows on his knees, his empty glass cradled loosely in his hands. "What difference does it make how you get your man, as long as you get him? Listen, if you ask me, you're doing old Cecil boy a favor. I don't exactly see the females of New Hope beating a path to his door. If it wasn't for your invitation this morning, he probably wouldn't have a thing to do all month."

Wendy figured Travis was probably underestimating the scholarly Cecil, but she had to agree that, in many respects, he was right about her.

So far she'd gone nearly thirty years and had yet to succeed in catching a mate. Obviously, when it came to captivating a man's attention, she was dropping the ball somewhere. With Travis there to guide her every step of the way with little cues, she could most likely come off as reasonably suave and sophisticated. Yes, she would exude self-confidence. She would be able to be the kind of woman an intelligent man like Cecil would be proud to call his wife. At least, she hoped so. This had to work. December first was approaching like a speeding train.

A quick glance at her watch told her that if she was going to complete her multitude of Sunday night chores and still make it to work bright and early tomorrow morning, she'd better get a move on. Stuffing her pad and pen into her purse, she began to gather her belongings and prepared to leave.

"Okay." She sighed as she stood and, reaching down, affectionately stroked Dusty's soft cheek. "I guess I'll see you guys tomorrow."

"Yeah. I'll pick you up in the morning," Travis agreed and, standing, walked her to the gate between their properties.

"Wendy, wait!" Dustin called, rushing after her, a large, colorful lollipop—looking only vaguely taste-tested—clutched in his sticky hand. "I saved this one for you," he said shyly, holding the candy out to her.

"Oh, sweet potato! These are my favorite," she crowed, taking his gift and drawing the beaming boy close. She smiled over his satiny soft, blond head at his father.

Travis looked on indulgently. Funny how Dusty had never given anything to BambiAnn.

* * *

After two busy days at the post office for both Wendy and Travis, Wednesday finally arrived. During the past two days—in the few spare moments they'd managed to grab together in the back room—they practiced their secret hand signals, leaving Wendy more confused and nervous than ever. Nevertheless, Travis insisted that it would behoove her to memorize the sign language and be prepared to use it. They also discussed their possible attire options for the evening, had a few impromptu dance sessions to the statically emanated tunes from the ancient radio Travis lugged from job to job, and managed, just barely, on more than one touch-and-go occasion, to avoid each other's lips.

But it wasn't easy.

Since Wendy had never experienced a kiss like the one she shared with Travis before, she was dying to see if her memory served her correctly. To see if it was really as thrilling and wonderful as she remembered.

Since Travis had experienced every kind of kiss before, except for the one he shared with Wendy, he was dying to see if his memory served him correctly. To see if Wendy had really spoiled him for any other woman's kiss in the future.

However, as much as both of them wanted to test their theories about each other's kiss, they each privately decided that it was in their own best interest to keep the dating lessons on a platonic level. They had to stay the course and work hard if Wendy was going to achieve her goal.

Travis hoped that he could forget the mind-bending sensations of Wendy's kiss, and stay out of her personal life. Teaching her to kiss was one thing. Getting hung up on her was another.

Wendy hoped—if she was lucky—that Cecil would kiss her good-night, and the wonderful, all-encompassing feeling of rapture that Travis had shown her would overtake her again. Most likely, she reasoned, it wasn't the *man* who'd kept her awake all week since her kissing lesson. It had to be the *kiss*. And if that was the case, Cecil's kiss would send her into orbit, too.

So, after two days of intense rehearsal, Wendy finally felt ready for bachelor number one. And, if all went well tonight and she and Cecil really hit it off, quite possibly they would attend the Russo wedding as an engaged couple. A shiver of anticipation ran up her spine at the thought, and in a flurry of excited activity, Wendy prepared for her evening with Cecil.

After spending the afternoon on the phone, consulting with Beth and Sue Ellen in between handing out stamps, Wendy finally decided that for this particular evening anyway, she would spread her own fashion wings. Armed with a stack of the latest glamour magazines, she headed to a local boutique after work and selected her wardrobe.

The soft black knit dress she chose was simple, no peek a boo holes or plunging necklines. However, it draped fetchingly over her slender figure, highlighting all of her best features, and the daring slit at the side showed plenty of sheer black stocking. Her shoes were simple black high heels, lending a shapely curve to her calves.

Once she arrived back at home, she carefully copied a hairstyle she liked from the cover of *Metropolitan*. Sweeping her sun blond tresses up into a loose pile of waves at her crown, she fashioned a simple knot and pulled several long, wavy strands down around her face to soften the effect. It was no floral centerpiece, but it would have to do. Some simple jewelry and light makeup were added to complete her look.

As she stood at her bedroom mirror, just before Travis arrived to pick her up, a host of last-minute doubts assailed her and chewed at her already nervous gut.

Oh, no! Her outfit was all wrong. She looked too plain. Heavens, she thought, wringing her hands. She should have picked up some fresh flowers for her hair. Put on some false eyelashes. Gotten a new pair of aquamarine contacts. How was she going to capture Cecil's attention if she blended into the woodwork?

Unfortunately, she was out of time. Travis hit the doorbell, and with what she was sure was an obligatory drop of the jaw and nod of approval, they were off to pick up Cecil and BambiAnn.

Travis was going to choke to death.

He wasn't sure why, exactly. Could be the gallon of eye-watering perfume that BambiAnn had felt necessary to dab behind each and every one of her throbbing pulse points. Could be the thick haze of cigar and cigarette smoke that hung in the air of Little Joe's Café on Wednesday night. Everyone celebrating the middle of the week. Then again, it could be the lump that had lodged in his throat the moment he'd laid eyes on Wendy as she'd opened her door to him earlier that evening.

Lord have mercy, he thought, training his eyes on her as she preceded him through the mob at Little Joe's, she was *stunning*. Somehow, she'd managed to hit her stride in the world of fashion because she looked so very...fine. Oh, yes. Damn fine indeed. She was far and away the classiest woman in the entire, standing-room-only Little Joe's Café.

However, at this point, the cause for his discomfort was irrelevant. Whatever the reason for the vicious irritant in his throat, if he didn't get something to drink soon, he was most certainly going to cough up a lung. Whipping a handkerchief from his hip pocket, he covered his mouth and gave in to the convulsive spasms that had his eyes running and him, gasping for air. Luckily, the other three in his party had moved ahead of him through the dimly lit room and into the throng. It gave him a chance to take in some much needed oxygen and mop his streaming eyes before he caught up with them.

"I love this band," BambiAnn simpered as the two couples reached one of the last empty tables near the dance floor. "I just love, love, love music, don't you?" she asked in her breathy Marilyn Monroe voice. She lowered her ample hips into the chair Travis held for her. "Ooo. I just love this place," she declared with a tinkling giggle and a shake of her platinum blond, bubble-do.

Wendy sighed. Perhaps she should have checked her brain at the door. Maybe then Cecil would find her as interesting as he seemed to find BambiAnn.

"Mmm," was all Travis was able to utter. He smiled as benignly as possible then nodded as he took the seat next to BambiAnn.

Smile plus nod equals laugh, Wendy chanted to herself as she caught these signals from Travis in her peripheral vision. Throwing back her head, she laughed as gaily as she could muster, considering the pounding headache BambiAnn's perfume had given her on the ride over. "Oh, yes. I love it, too," Wendy agreed, laughing gaily once more. Man, if she didn't get some aspirin soon, her head was going to cave in. "I love, love, love music." Copying the effervescent BambiAnn, Wendy smiled beguilingly at Cecil and added that she loved all kinds of music, this music in particular, and loved the song that they were playing now.

Whatever it was.

Actually, she'd never heard it before, but she refrained from adding that tidbit. Once again, she tossed back her head and joined BambiAnn in some tinkling laughter. Although, what in the heck was so funny was beyond her. She laughed with what she prayed was carefree abandon at something Cecil was saying about how he, too, loved this song. They were all in agreement it seemed, Wendy thought, still laughing through her gritted teeth.

At Travis's quizzically arched brow and the slight censorious shake of his head, she stopped laughing and shrugged. What was with him? she wondered defensively. Hadn't he just cued her to laugh gaily? And why was he blinking so rapidly at her that way? She didn't remember rehearsing that signal.

Cecil held her chair for her, then taking his own, settled in next to her. "Come here often?" he inquired politely after he was able to drag his eyes away from BambiAnn.

Wendy hoped her laughter was as breathy and tinkling as BambiAnn's. "Oh, no." She shot a furtive glance at Travis for direction. What should she say now? Cecil must be wondering how she could love a place that she never frequented. Travis coughed a deep, racking cough.

Hmm, Wendy mused. Travis was coughing. What did that mean again?

Cecil smoothed his thinning, sandy blond hair back away from his high, shiny forehead. "Oh," he said pleasantly, then glanced with concern at Travis.

BambiAnn patted Travis on the back and snuggled close, clasping his biceps amongst her generous cleavage. "Ooo. Are you all right, sugarpie?" she breathed huskily.

"Fine," Travis gasped, his eyes burning and watering as BambiAnn's perfume succeeded in laminating his throat tightly closed. Whatever she was wearing tonight, it was new and it was strong. It smelled vaguely familiar and he was reasonably sure he had something just like it in the garage that he used for killing weeds.

Clawing at his lucky bolo tie, he unbuttoned his shirt and scratched at the tingling rash that was radiating up his neck and spreading to his face.

A small crease furrowed between Wendy's brows as she tried to sort out the multitude of secret signals that swirled through her brain. Travis had scratched his jaw, meaning she should ask Cecil to help her with her chair. But, that couldn't be right. She was already sitting down. Unless . . . He must mean he wanted her to ask Cecil to help her with her wrap. Glancing down at her light evening cape, she thrust it out to Cecil with what she hoped was a breathy, dewy-lipped, gregarious BambiAnn-type smile.

His answering smile was puzzled as he took it from her, examined it, complimented her on it, then handed it back.

Okay, she decided, laughing gaily as she quickly stuffed her cape down on the floor by her feet, she'd muffed that one. No matter. By Travis's insistent cough, she could tell it was time to move on. *Let's see . . .* She pursed her lips in concentration. *Coughing, coughing, coughing.* Coughing equaled . . . blow in his ear.

He wanted her to blow in Cecil's ear? Now? Already? Tightening her grip on her chair, she stared intently at Travis. Well, she guessed so. The way he was coughing, one would think that if she didn't blow in Cecil's ear pretty soon, the world might end. Licking her lips, she took a covert peek at Cecil.

He was peering thoughtfully at the small specials menu that was lodged between the salt and pepper shakers, his pointed features knitted in concentration. Travis had told her to trust him on this, but for pity's sake, shouldn't she work up to this moment?

Although, maybe he had a point, she mused thoughtfully. BambiAnn was already busy nuzzling Travis's neck and ears as he sent frantic, secret signals for her into his handkerchief.

She gave her head a slight shake. No wonder she'd never gotten anywhere with a serious relationship, she thought self-deprecatingly. In her ignorance, she would have saved the blowing-in-the-ear thing for later. But here she could see for herself, thanks to BambiAnn's flamboyant demonstration, that blowing in the ear came into play right off the bat. Who'd have thought? Men were such funny creatures. Did they really enjoy having air blown into their ears? She sighed. It was all so complicated. Gathering her nerve before she could lose it, she leaned over and blew a quick puff of air into Cecil's ear.

Cecil glanced up from his perusal of the menu and frowned uncertainly at her.

Uh-oh, she thought, panicking. What now? "I, uh..." She darted a help-me glance at Travis who had finally stopped coughing and was now winking uncontrollably at her. This stupid signal game would be the death of her. "Hi, there," she breathed in her best BambiMarilyn impression, as she tried to remember what winking signified.

"Hello," Cecil returned nervously and dabbed at his beet red ears with his napkin.

Wendy gnawed on her lower lip. She wasn't exactly batting a thousand here, but she supposed these things took time. Like it or not, she would have to trust Travis and his signals. Obviously, with his dating track record, he knew what he was doing. The way BambiAnn was making a production of fawning all over him told her that much.

The band sawed its way through one rollicking country-western song after another, and Wendy watched as two by two, the many patrons of Little Joe's threaded their way around the large wooden dance floor. And, if Wendy wasn't an absolute nervous wreck over the success of this double date, she'd most likely be delighting in the earthy Western ambience. Popular café by day, New Hope hot spot by night, the place had become a roaring success.

Through the billowing clouds of smoke, their waiter finally appeared to take their drink orders. Wendy ordered ice tea. BambiAnn ordered a Shirley Temple. Cecil liked the sound of that and ordered the same.

Travis wished for a canister of oxygen, but ordered a glass of water instead. He clenched his jaw. The way BambiAnn was hanging all over him was driving him crazy. Trying not to let his rotten mood show, he shrugged and pulled back from her annoying ministrations to his neck. Sometimes she just didn't know when to quit. Like now, for instance, he thought, his irritation growing as he lifted and dropped his shoulders again.

He could sense Wendy watching them, and felt suddenly conspicuous. He didn't want BambiAnn to set a bad example for her. This was not the way he wanted her to learn to act on a date. Wendy was a lady with an innate sense of class. She should trust her own intuition, not copy BambiAnn's ostentatious style.

Drawing her cheek between her back teeth, Wendy read— and reread—Travis's signals. *Ask Cecil to dance,* he was telegraphing with his shoulders. Well... okay. Personally, she felt that the question of dancing was a bit premature— especially since the band had just taken a break and the dance floor had cleared—but vowing to trust Travis, she turned and bestowed the reserved Cecil with a seductive smile.

"Would you care to dance, Cecil?" she breathed and twittered brainlessly.

Oh, how she longed to toss off this phony act and just be her regular, boring self. But she couldn't. Not if she wanted to beat the odds and land a man by her birthday.

Startled, Cecil reddened and glanced out to the empty dance floor. "Uh, no, thank you," he demurred.

Travis, feeling his throat closing again, shrugged violently, urging BambiAnn to give him some air.

"Travis," BambiAnn reproached, her girlish voice husky. "You don't have to be such a...a..." She pouted prettily as she thought. "Big meanie." Insulted, she scooted away from him and dealt with his rejection by batting her spiky lashes at Cecil.

Wendy focused all her concentration on reading Travis's vehement shrugs. Gracious, he certainly was adamant about wanting her to dance with Cecil, she thought, somewhat perplexed. Perhaps he could sense that Cecil needed coaxing. She arranged her lips into a playful pout, like the one Cecil seemed to be admiring so much on BambiAnn. "Are you sure?" She laughed gaily for good measure. "I just love this song," she cajoled, indicating the soft elevator music that filtered through the speakers while the band took five.

"Uh, no, thank you."

"Oh, come on now, Cecil. It will be fun." She hoped she sounded convincing, although dancing sans band with the reticent Cecil was quickly losing its appeal. She wished Travis would stop pushing her this way. The pressure was getting to her.

"No." Cecil was polite but firm.

Luckily the waiter arrived to take their dinner order, saving Wendy from having to drag the killjoy Cecil out to the floor. She breathed a sigh of relief, grateful for the reprieve. This snaring-a-man business was exhausting. Not to mention loathsome.

Too bad she couldn't just skip the mating rituals and go straight to marriage. Do not pass Go. Do not collect two hundred dollars. Although, she had to admit, she was beginning to have her doubts about Cecil. He was nowhere near as much fun as Travis. Not that that mattered, she amended to herself. But, hey, if she had to set up housekeeping with someone, she should at least enjoy his company.

The waiter jotted down their selections, collected their menus and disappeared back into the smog from whence he'd come.

Travis snatched several napkins from the dispenser on the table and dabbed at his burning eyes. He'd never experienced an allergic reaction so severe before. His sinuses felt as if they were ready to blast off. Pinching the bridge of his aching nose, he tried to smile at his pouting date.

Oh, for crying in the night. Wendy grimaced as Travis pinched the bridge of his nose. Couldn't he give her a moment to recover from Cecil's embarrassing announcement that he had no desire to dance before he had her throw herself at the poor man?

Obviously not, she thought disgustedly and, copying BambiAnn's affected giggle the best she could, inched her chair closer to Cecil's. Unfortunately, much to her chagrin, Cecil adjusted his seat away from her. Sighing, she watched as Travis vigorously massaged the bridge of his nose, winking and blinking all the while.

Stoically gripping the arms of her chair, she set out after Cecil. According to Travis, it was time to reach out and adjust Cecil's collar—laughing gaily while she did it, of course. This was an especially difficult task, considering Cecil wore a crewneck. And darn it, anyway, she thought as Travis continued his infernal signals, just how close did he expect her to sit? The way he was trying to pinch his nose off made it seem like he wouldn't be happy until she was sitting on poor Cecil's delicate lap. The very thought was unnerving. The closer she got to Cecil, the farther away she wished she was.

Travis had said "be aggressive," but honestly. This was getting ridiculous. Besides, Cecil didn't seem to be enjoying her advances the way Travis had promised he would. Was this part of the game? Was he playing hard to get? Oh, well. Time was short.

In four short weeks she would be thirty, and—she thought with determination—engaged to be married.

Leaning closer still to Cecil, she closed her eyes and blew into his ear.

The food finally arrived and as the evening progressed, it seemed to Wendy that no matter how close she snuggled up to Cecil, no matter how gaily she laughed, no matter how many questions she pelted the poor man with, no matter how often she blew in his ear, it wasn't enough for Travis. Honestly, she thought, pretending to listen to some dull thing or another Cecil was saying to BambiAnn, the man was a slave driver.

The coughing and scratching and winking and shrugging.... She was about ready to lose what was left of her mind, trying to keep up with his rapid-fire instructions. If catching a husband took this much effort, Wendy was beginning to think she'd rather stay single.

Especially if it meant spending the rest of her life with the tedious Cecil.

He was a crashing bore. Although, Wendy had to admit, it wasn't entirely his fault. The way Travis kept signaling her to steer the conversation back to him, it was understandable that he would drone endlessly on about himself. At least BambiAnn seemed riveted to his conversation. Amazing. She'd never have taken BambiAnn for the computer groupie type.

Sighing, Wendy leaned back in her chair, away from Cecil's bony body. She'd learned one interesting fact about herself tonight. She didn't like skinny men. If—she thought, watching Cecil natter on at BambiAnn—by the apparently minuscule chance that she and Cecil should end up together, her first project would be fattening him up.

She preferred her men with a little meat on their bones. Kind of like Travis, she noted, her eyes straying toward where he sat across from her. She admired the way his muscles flexed and bulged beneath his Western-style shirt as he listened to Cecil drone on. Yes, Travis was someone she could get into snuggling up against.

That is, of course, if he were husband material. Which he wasn't. Life was so unfair. Guessing that no one would miss her if she went to powder her nose, she excused herself from the table and headed toward the ladies' room.

Every blasted man in the place had danced with her. Every blasted man, with the exception of the two she'd come with, Travis thought churlishly as he watched Wendy showing off the dance steps he'd taught her with her latest partner, Conway Brubaker. She'd gotten up over an hour ago— to powder her nose, she'd claimed—and never come back, leaving him here alone with SuperNerd and BambiAnn. Was she trying to make Cecil jealous? Well, it wasn't working. It was, however, Travis noted disgruntledly as he drummed his fingers impatiently on the tabletop, irritating the hell out of him.

Why wasn't Cecil out there fighting for his woman? What the hell was wrong with him? he wondered in disgust as the twerp stared moonily at BambiAnn and blathered endlessly on about himself. Wendy had created a monster with all her outrageous behavior.

For the life of him, he couldn't figure out what had gotten into her tonight, what with the flirting, and questions and breathy laughter and the flamboyant caressing of Cecil's bony body. The way she acted, the twerp had a better build than Stallone. Surely, she couldn't be serious.

It was almost as if Wendy was doing her best to emulate BambiAnn. Copying every feeble trick in BambiAnn's book. And on her, it didn't look good. Made him want to punch someone. Someone like . . . Cecil Yates.

Or Conway Brubaker. Right now, Wendy and Conway were busy putting the stars of *Dirty Dancing* to shame, with their handsy, grabby, happy, twirly-whirly dancing style. Looked like she might lose her precious chastity out there on the dance floor, the way she was bumping and grinding with old Conway Baryshnikov. Travis took an angry swig of his beer. He had a fancy move or two he'd like to try out on Brubaker's face.

After tonight, he would see to it that she scratched both Cecil Yates and Conway Brubaker off her list of suitors. As far as Travis was concerned, neither of them was husband material. Brubaker was a pretty boy, womanizing wild man, whose only redeeming quality was the fact that he could outdance Patrick Swayze. And Yates—Travis trained a bleary, weary eye on the little goober across the table—was a twerp.

Yeah, he thought, watching the male population of Little Joe's Café salivate like Pavlov's dogs over *his* neighbor, it was time to rethink the "list." Wendy needed to find a regular guy to date. Some guy who would be a decent fa-

.ther to her kids. Some guy she could relax with. Just be herself with. Some guy who liked her just the way she was. Not some jackass who could only see a pile of wavy blond hair and a pair of killer legs under her new postal hot pants.

Pulling himself out of his ruminations long enough to re-fill his glass from the pitcher he was making every effort to kill, he managed to notice that Yates and BambiAnn had left. Together. There they went, he thought as he watched them disappear without so much as a so-long-see-ya-'bye, past the dance floor, around the band, through the sea of humanity and out the front door. BambiAnn looked like the cat that had swallowed the canary. And Yates...well, Yates looked like a million-dollar canary.

Well, Travis mused, lifting his beer in salute, at least the evening had one bright spot.

8

→ ←

The crisp, cool night air felt wonderful on Wendy's flushed and overheated cheeks as she walked across her front yard to her porch. Travis had let her out in his driveway and then pulled the truck into his garage. They had picked up Dusty from Faith's house where the boy had spent the evening, and Travis was probably tucking him in at the moment. She could see the night-light in Dusty's room from where she stood in front of her house, only a few yards away. A small, tender smile graced her lips. Though they'd lifted him out of his bed in Faith's spare room and driven him all the way across town, Dusty hadn't even stirred.

It was nearly one in the morning, but she didn't feel a bit tired. She could have danced all night and—if Travis hadn't reminded her that she had to be at work at 8:00 a.m.—she would have. She couldn't remember ever having had quite that much fun. Deep down, in her heart of hearts, she wished that Travis would have pulled his sour face out of his glass long enough to ask her to dance. But since neither he nor Cecil had seemed inclined to cut a rug, she'd taken the opportunity to get to know a number of New Hope's eligible bachelors.

She took a deep breath of fresh air. If it hadn't been so late—or early, she mused, glancing at her watch—she would have burst into song. It was wonderful to be alive. The small waterfall that Travis had installed near her front porch the year before burbled pleasantly as she slung her purse onto the stairs and plopped down next to it. There were a billion twinkling stars in the clear, black Texas sky, and leaning on her elbows, Wendy tilted her head back and spent several long moments reveling in their beauty.

"Why aren't you in bed?" The sultry question came from Travis as he lowered himself next to her on the steps.

A riot of gooseflesh broke out on her arms and legs. Wendy slowly pulled her gaze from the heavens and trained it on him. "Because I'm not tired," she murmured. Her eyes flashed to her feet and she smiled. "My feet, on the other hand, have laid down and died." Pushing herself to an upright position, she reached down, unbuckled her pumps, and slipped them off her aching feet then began to massage her toes.

Travis stretched his own booted feet out in front of him and crossed his legs at the ankles. "Yeah. Mine, too."

"Yours?" Wendy giggled. "Why do your feet hurt? You didn't get up once the entire evening." Unfastening the clip that held her hair at the top of her head, she gave her head a vigorous shake and sent her hair floating around her shoulders.

His eyes, dark and mysterious in the ethereal light of the moon, caressed her, and without warning he reached up and grasped a handful of her hair, letting it trail through his fingers. As if suddenly realizing where he was and who he was with, he dropped his hand. "Yeah, well, I noticed you didn't sit down once the entire evening, either," he remarked.

Tossing her hair over her shoulder, her dimples appeared. "I had a ball. You know, I think I danced with every man in the place tonight, except for Cecil." She pulled her lower lip between her teeth. "And you," she amended.

Travis harrumphed. "So I noticed."

Arching a quizzical brow, Wendy hiked the hem of her black knit skirt a little higher on her thigh and began to unfasten the garters that had held her stockings up. Beth had talked her into these uncomfortable things. Said they drove men wild. She darted a quick glance at Travis. If the glazed look on his face as he watched her roll her stocking down her leg was any indication, Beth had been right. Suddenly, Wendy felt a heady power that she'd never felt before. A feminine power. A sexual power. Her heart picked up speed.

"Well," she said, tugging the nylon off and tossing it up on the porch behind her, "if you wanted to dance so badly, you should have said something. Besides, I don't know what you're so grumpy about. I'm the one who should be mad." Reaching under her other thigh, she unfastened the remaining garter. "All those crazy secret signals of yours drove poor Cecil right out the door." Giggling, she gathered her hem into her hand and moved it out of her way as she began to remove her second stocking.

Travis cleared his throat. "Uh," he began, dragging his eyes away from her legs and giving his head a slight shake. "What signals?" His voice sounded strained.

Sighing, Wendy stopped rolling her nylon at midcalf and narrowed her eyes in suspicion. "All the secret signals you made me practice. You know, the winking, the shrugging, the coughing." She looked expectantly at him. Why was he being so obtuse? She laughed. "Good heavens, the way you were carrying on tonight, if I hadn't known better, I'd have thought you were having some sort of fit." Giggling good-naturedly, she went back to removing her stocking. She could afford to be in a good mood. She might have lost Cecil, but she gained about twenty other admirers.

None of them screamed husband material, but, hey, more than likely, many of them were just diamonds in the rough. She knew she'd have to kiss a few frogs before she found her prince. Cecil had definitely turned out to be a frog. Flinging the other stocking over her shoulder, she smiled up at Travis. Travis on the other hand, was no frog.

Land-o'-goshin. He was a handsome devil. Out of all the men she'd danced with that night, not one had made her feel the way Travis could make her feel with a simple look. Although, the look he was giving her now was anything but simple.

She dropped her eyes, following the movement of his arms as he folded them across his chest, then lifted her gaze back to his face. He was the perfect combination of manly and boyish good looks. His hollow cheeks gave rise to nicely sculpted bones, which melded into a square jaw and chiseled chin. It was the kind of face that would look at home behind a boardroom desk or under the hood of a car.

Handsome, but not too pretty. With the possible exception of his eyes. He had light gray eyes that could penetrate a woman's soul. And, his lashes. They were the kind of thick, long, dark eyelashes that Sue Ellen would kill for. Wendy smiled. She was just glad Sue Ellen hadn't gotten hold of Travis's gorgeous hair. Her eyes strayed to his heavy brown hair. It looked black in the moonlight.

Yes, indeed. Travis was no frog. She sighed with regret. Cecil had left before she'd had the opportunity to test her kissing theory. Not that she particularly wanted to kiss Cecil, but she was dying to find out if it was kissing in general that had her senses exploding with ecstasy, or if it was the man. Specifically—Travis.

He was looking at her as if she'd gone around the bend.

"I didn't send you any signals," he informed her, resting his chin on his chest and peering through the darkness at her as she trailed her toes in the small waterfall beside her steps.

"You didn't?"

"No."

"Then what was all that coughing about?"

"I was having an allergic reaction to that embalming fluid BambiAnn called perfume."

Wendy stared at him, her eyes round. "Is that why you were pinching your nose and shrugging and coughing and—"

"Gasping for air. Yes." Travis nodded and returned her wide grin. "You thought I was sending you signals?" he asked, incredulous.

"Well, for pity's sake, of course I did. The way you insisted that we practice them and all, I thought you wanted me to use them. All evening."

Travis hooted. "So that explains why you were chasing old Cecil around the table in your chair. I wondered why you were so tenacious with him. Like a dog with an old shoe."

Dragging her toe through the small pool, Wendy sent a spray of water splashing across Travis's leg. "I beg your pardon," she cried, feigning insult. "A *dog* with an old *shoe?*"

"Well..." He laughed. "Yeah. I can't believe you thought I was cueing you to stick your feet in his lap and run your hands through his hair that way." His laughter shook her front steps.

"Weren't you?" She giggled.

"No!" He wiped his eyes. "I was trying to breathe."

"Oh." Wendy began to laugh in earnest. "So, I wasn't supposed to be blowing in his ear right off the bat?" she choked.

"Oh, man," Travis howled and, sitting up, clutched at his gut. "You thought I was telling you to..." He was rendered silent for a moment by the hilarious thought. "*Blow in his ear? Right there at the table?*" Slapping his thighs, he hung his head between his legs and gave in to the swells of laughter that crowded his throat. Oh, it was too much. The image of the prissy Cecil, and the strange look of shock and discomfort he wore all evening. It was all making perfect sense.

He could feel Wendy's slight body leaning against his arm, shaking along with him, seeing the humor in the situation. She was such a good sport. Most women he knew would be shooting him dead about now.

Pulling his head up, he dared to take a peek at Wendy, and seeing her cheeks streaming with tears of laughter sent him over the edge once again.

"I...I..." She gasped. "I thought you wanted me to force him to dance, the way you were shrugging your shoulders that way. I thought...you...ha!—knew what you were... *doing!*" she screamed and fell across his lap.

"Well, that explains the yellow pallor in his cheeks," Travis groaned, breathing deeply with Wendy as she struggled back to an upright position. "You know," he told her, when he could finally speak again, "while you were out dancing..." He reached up and ran a hand across his mouth to stem the impending tidal wave of mirth. "BambiAnn wanted to know why you were interrogating poor Cecil that way. She said she thought you were..." He started to laugh again. "Scaring him half to death with all your questions and demands."

"*My* questions and demands?" Wendy shrieked, doubling over. "*You* were the one who suggested I draw him out. 'People *love* that,'" she mimicked, her face scrunched with glee.

"You drew him out, all right. Right out of the room."

"I know." Wendy hiccuped and sighed. "I saw them leave together. Travis..." Dabbing at her cheeks with her sleeve, she grew suddenly sober. "I'm so sorry. I hope you're okay." Her voice was gentle. Tender. Filled with compassion.

"Oh, don't worry about it," he said, and smiled, inordinately pleased at her concern. "I've been meaning to call it quits with BambiAnn for quite a while now, and I think she knew it. We were never all that serious." Leaning back on one elbow, he reached up and playfully tugged a lock of her hair. "Actually, I think BambiAnn and Cecil make a pretty good couple. She was extremely impressed with his income figures, and he seemed to be pretty impressed with her... figure, too." He grinned. "To tell you the truth, I'm relieved."

She drew her lower lip between her straight, white teeth, worrying it. "Really?"

He nodded. "Really. When I decide to get married again, I want it to be to someone that Dusty loves as much as I do." He studied her for her reaction.

Sitting up straight, Wendy tugged her hem down over her knees and locked her arms at her shins. "That's good," she agreed with relief, nodding solemnly. "And it's not like you don't have a whole slew of women you can fall back on."

He nodded. "Yeah." Right about now, he'd like to fall back on her, he thought, dropping his eyes to the lower lip she'd been so thoughtfully chewing a moment ago. A primal, sexual urge began to stir low in his gut. He was growing to need her. And want her. He hadn't wanted anyone this way for a long time. Absently, he wondered why it didn't scare the hell out of him. "And I'm sorry it didn't work out for you with Cecil." He dropped this platitude for her benefit, but knew it was a barefaced lie. Truthfully, he was glad the little weasel had taken off with BambiAnn. Killed two birds with one stone, in his opinion.

"Oh, that's okay." Wendy shrugged and rested her chin on her knees. Smiling, she angled her cheek to face him. "I don't think Cecil was exactly my soul mate. With or without the secret signals."

Travis felt a slow smile steal across his hardened heart. "No."

"That's okay. I had a lot of fun tonight, in spite of all the mixed messages." She giggled. "I just don't know how I'm ever going to face Cecil again." Slanting her head, her gaze collided with his. "I want to thank you for teaching me to dance, Travis. I had no idea how much fun dancing could be. Especially dancing with someone as good as Conway Brubaker. No wonder Sue Ellen calls him Conway Swayze. He's wonderful. And," she sighed, "handsome."

Travis was sure his heart stopped beating.

Wendy lazily studied his face. *Not as handsome as you*, she wanted to say, but couldn't. Travis would think she'd lost her mind if she confessed to her burgeoning crush on him. What a goon she was. Going and getting all hung up on him over one little kiss. She wasn't supposed to be thinking about the soft caress of his lips. No. She should be concentrating on someone else's lips. Someone like... Conway Brubaker. Taking a deep breath, she made a decision to confide her secret in Travis. "You know," she began shyly, "when I was slow dancing with Conway, for a minute there, I thought he might kiss me."

This was it. Call the cardio unit, Travis thought, panic clutching at his chest. "Really." The calm, steady sound of his voice surprised him.

"Mmm-hmm," she admitted, nodding. "I kind of wished he would."

Over my dead body, he thought, suddenly hating the handsome Conway with a passion. He tried to shake it off, but couldn't. The volatile passion that exploded between him and Wendy when they kissed was his, dammit. Not Conway Brubaker's. Jealously, unwanted and unaccustomed, tore him up inside. "Why is that?" he asked, a grim muscle throbbing in his jaw.

"Mmm..." She hesitated, then, squeezing her eyes tightly shut, forged ahead. "I wanted to see if kissing another man would be as... exciting as kissing you." She ducked her head, embarrassed. "I know that you've probably already forgotten that we kissed after our practice date, but for me, it was kind of a big deal."

Travis felt his heart resume beating again. In fact, it began to race.

Toying with a lock of her hair, Wendy continued with her admission. "I haven't had much experience kissing, and I know I need more practice before I kiss someone as handsome and experienced and worldly as Conway Brubaker—"

His heart stopped again.

"In fact," she confessed, humiliation coloring her words, "you were my first really...um, passionate kiss."

His heart started again.

Although he was bothered by her plans to hone her kissing expertise on Conway "The Playboy" Brubaker, he was relieved and thrilled to learn that he had been her first. Something poignant swelled in his throat as he watched her face. It was such a sweet face. Classically beautiful, yet filled with wonderful emotion that made her unique. Amazing how he'd never noticed how lovely she was before she'd started this husband hunt of hers. Any fool could see that she was a beauty, inside and out. Any fool, but him. He guessed he couldn't see past BambiAnn's voluptuous glamour girl act.

Slowly, he reached out and cupped her soft, delicate cheek in his work-roughened palm. Their eyes tangled and danced, suddenly seeing things in each other that they had never noticed before. Drawing her inexorably closer, Travis lowered his mouth to hers for the slowest, sweetest, softest kiss he'd ever experienced.

Like angel's wings, he imagined as his lips moved lightly over hers, hovering, touching, lightly tasting. She parted her lips, ever so slightly, and he could feel her warm, sweet breath in his mouth. She tasted of sunshine and rainbows and bubbling waterfalls and—sighing, he deepened the kiss—yonder light. Man. The things she did to him. Never had he kissed a woman this way. The ecstasy was indescribable. Her lashes, whisper-soft, tickled his cheek, and Travis, if it hadn't been for the paper boy's misplaced aim, would have thought he'd ascended to an alternate planet again. The Technicolor passion planet.

The dull thud of the paper, as it bounced off the back of his head and landed on the lawn, pulled Travis back to reality.

Wendy lay curled in his lap, his shirt twisted into wads under her tightly clenched fists. How she'd ended up in this position, he'd never know. Pulling her forehead to his lips, he planted a proprietary kiss and murmured into her hair.

"I don't want you kissing Conway Brubaker." His tone brooked no argument. He didn't want her kissing anyone, but that wasn't realistic. No. Realistically, she should probably kiss a bunch of guys before she got engaged. He just didn't want to know about it. He didn't want to have to listen to her accounts of her various good-night kisses. He was getting too involved as it was. This was not good for either of them. It was time to cut her loose. Resting his chin at the top of her head, he leaned back with her on the stairs. "I think you're ready to solo," he said flatly.

"Really? You think I'm ready to go out with someone by myself?"

He exhaled mightily. "Yeah." Closing his eyes, he added, "Anyone but Conway Brubaker."

9

Beads of perspiration broke out on Travis's brow as he savagely attacked the offending hedge with swift, powerful strokes of his long-handled garden shears. Because of his procrastination, the paint job on his poor truck bore permanent scars. Well, enough was enough. He wasn't going to put up with this irritating situation another minute. No way. Travis had been meaning to trim back the giant laurel hedge between his and Wendy's driveways for a long time now.

He just hadn't meant to accomplish this task at midnight.

But what better time to do it? he wondered, wrestling the heavy, tangled undergrowth into the middle of his driveway. Dusty was sound asleep and out of harm's way, he thought logically as he kicked and punched the growing mountain of hedge clippings out from under his feet. It was cool outside, so he wouldn't get overheated, he rationalized, huffing and puffing as he mopped his sweaty face with the sleeve of his raggedy old flannel shirt.

And, he could keep an eye out for Wendy.

Much to his chagrin, she had taken him up on his suggestion and was out on her first solo date, while he spent the evening acting like a worried father. No, that wasn't quite true. A worried father wouldn't feel the searing sense of jealousy that whirled through his gut like a twister on the rampage. No, he was acting more like a worried lunatic.

Pushing the branches of the hedge aside for the umpteenth time that evening, he peered through the darkness across Wendy's yard and checked to see if she had somehow magically appeared on her front porch. But no. She was still out, doing heaven only knew what with mystery date number two. Abner Perkins.

Abner was one of Travis's subcontractors. Seemed like a nice enough guy. Okay, admittedly, Abner had a few problems, but who didn't? Wendy, the lady that she was, wasn't one to hold a person's little idiosyncrasies against them. At least he hoped not, since it was his idea in the first place that she call Abner and make a date.

Good old Abner. About six feet. And that was just his belt measurement. Interesting thing about Abner, Travis mused. It seemed he always carried leftovers from his meal somewhere in his longish beard. Because Abner was such a sensitive soul, no one wanted to point this little problem out. So, Abner would go through the day with crumbs of this and that dangling from his face, bobbing distractingly as he spoke.

With a rueful smile, Travis shook his head and pushed his sweat soaked hair out of his face. Wendy had been yapping for the last three days about how she felt the need to kiss another man. Said she needed to do some comparison shopping, so to speak.

Why on earth she'd feel the need for that was beyond him. He knew she could search the world over and never find, with another living soul, what happened between them when their lips met. It just wasn't possible that something so...*incredible* could happen for her with another man. He'd been able to tell from the instant their mouths melded that first time that they had something special. Magical. Explosive. The mere thought of that kiss made his blood run hot.

Abner was a lucky son of a gun, getting a date with Wendy. In his opinion, good old Abner wasn't anywhere near Wendy's league, socially speaking. Funny, but if someone would have asked him last month, he'd have thought they were perfect for each other. Now though—he shook his head, tsk-tsking under his breath—now he had other ideas. When it came to Wendy, like his son before him, he'd seen the light. Sighing, he heaved a laurel branch as thick as his arm over his shoulder.

He'd suggested the less than attractive Abner to Wendy, mainly because he hoped when the date ended, she wouldn't feel like kissing him good-night. If, he thought peevishly, the damn date ever ended.

Picking up his clippers, Travis viciously whacked off a short, stubby branch that protruded into the drive. For Pete's sake, it had to be at least one in the morning. Travis angled his wrist to catch the glow of the overhead street lamp. One-seventeen. Where the hell was she? It was one-the-hell-seventeen in the morning. What was she doing? He closed his eyes. He couldn't think about it. If she was kissing Abner.... The very thought made him want to lash out.

Just as Travis was really getting into his frenzied assault on his monster foliage, a bright pair of headlights swung around the corner and into their cul-de-sac. Not wanting to be discovered for fear Wendy would get the wrong idea and think he was more concerned about her than he actually was, he dropped his clippers and dove headlong into the middle of the huge, overgrown hedge.

Aw, geez. This was not a good idea, he thought, feeling like a human shish kebab as the hedge held him aloft in its midst with dozens of pointy branches. However, it was too late to do anything about it now. Pulling a particularly sharp branch out of the middle of his back, Travis angled his head among the leaves so that he could see Abner and Wendy as they stepped out of the car and strolled right past him up the front steps to the door.

Even though he lay as still as humanly possible, the rustling leaves and snapping branches obscured their conversation. Shoot, he thought, holding his breath and straining to hear their murmured words. What on earth was Abner saying to Wendy? Whatever it was, she was smiling brightly and looking up at him with what he could only guess was adoration.

Travis felt suddenly nauseated. He might not be able to hear the words, but he could see Abner preparing for the move.

The *move*.

It was obvious. He was going to kiss her. Aw, criminy. And she was going to let him? Yeesh.

To Travis's eternal disgust, Abner pulled her into the meaty circle of his arms, much the way Travis had shown her one of her dates would, and planted a big, wet one somewhere in the vicinity of her lips. Travis blanched. He couldn't look. As quietly as he could, he twisted away from the unnerving scene before him and settled in to wait for Abner to take a hike.

At least he'd better be leaving, Travis fumed. If he thought he was coming in for a cup of coffee on the first date, he had another think coming. Travis knew how the male mind operated. Abner only wanted one thing, and he wasn't going to get it. Not here, not tonight. Not after they were engaged, not even after they were married. Not ever, if Travis could help it. A large supporting bough suddenly broke and Travis felt himself fall further into the dank and crawly recesses of his hedge.

Wendy pushed against Abner's doughy chest, relieved to have a reason to distract him. "Did you hear that?"

"Hear...what?" Abner's eyes were glazed, much like the pile of donuts he'd consumed for dessert. He reached for her.

Taking a step back, Wendy frowned. "That noise. It sounded like it was coming from the hedge."

Abner dropped his arms. "Probably just an animal."

"Yes, you're most likely right. Anyway," Wendy said brightly, smiling up at Abner, hoping she was effectively masking her revulsion, "thanks so much for a lovely evening." She decided to skip Travis's advice about saying how they ought to do it again sometime. Because there wouldn't be a next time. Not if she had anything to say about it.

"You bet," Abner said, shuffling his feet back and forth, his eyes shifting about as he nervously stroked his sticky beard.

Obviously, he was trying to find the words to ask her out again, and Wendy decided to head him off at the pass. "Gosh, Abner! Will you look at the time? It's after one-thirty in the morning! I have to get up in just a few short hours if I'm going to make it to church by first service. Well, you drive careful, now, you hear? And—" The words tumbled out in a rush as she ushered Abner back toward his car and opened the door for him. "Thank you again for the lovely…uh, all that food. I had a full—uh, fun time…there, uh, eating with you. So, again…" She closed the door after the nervous Abner, and patted the roof of the car. "Thanks for everything. Bye-bye," she chirped, and walked quickly back toward the sidewalk.

As if not knowing exactly what had hit him, Abner started his engine and waved uncertainly at Wendy. "'Bye, now," he called, slowly pulling away from the curb. Tooting his horn against the silent night, he rounded the corner and headed home.

Sighing, Wendy returned his wave and watched as his taillights disappeared from view.

"You can come out now, Travis," she called over her shoulder and into the hedge. "Travis," she repeated after a moment. "I know you're in there. You can stop spying on me and go to bed now."

The snap, crackle and pop of the laurel hedge that separated their driveways finally gave birth to Travis as he thrashed his way out of his hiding place.

"I wasn't spying on you," he protested testily as he staggered to his feet and dusted himself off. He gestured to his mountain of yard debris. "As you can see, I've been working on the hedge."

Wendy laughed. "From the inside out? At one-thirty in the morning, no less? Sure." She snorted. "You were spying on me, and you know it. Why don't you just admit it?"

He glared at her through narrowed eyes. "Hey, I'm a busy man. I don't have all day to work in my yard, like some people. I have to do it when I have the time."

What was stuck in his craw? Wendy wondered as she watched him yank off his leather gloves and fire them at the ground.

"But," he snapped, moving toward her, his eyes glittering dangerously in the lamplight, "since you seem so curious about whether or not I got an eyeful, I can tell you right here and now that you handled that good-night kiss all wrong."

Wendy smirked. "Oh, I did, did I?"

"Yes." He took a step closer and she could feel his heavy breath warm on her cheek. "You were acting completely disinterested."

"Because I *was* disinterested," she said, gazing up into the black depths of his eyes.

A muscle worked in his jaw, even as the worry in his eyes relaxed slightly. Reaching out, Travis grasped her upper arms and scowled as he pulled her tightly into his chest. "Wendy." Her name was a frustrated groan low in his throat. "If you're going to be engaged by the Russo wedding, you're going to have to act interested in a good-night kiss. Very interested."

She rested her palms against the steel hills of his broad chest and could feel the arrhythmic beat of his pulse.

Clutching his shirt for balance, she touched her upper lip with the tip of her tongue. *I'm interested.* The unspoken words swirled dizzily through her brain as her eyes locked in an electrical storm with his. *I'm very interested.*

With no time for vacillation or excuses, Travis pulled her mouth beneath his. Once again their lips had ignition and they were both blasted into orbit by a power that came only from the energy the two of them could generate together. Waves of gooseflesh raced up and down Wendy's arms and legs as she thrilled and shivered under the overwhelming onslaught. Kissing Abner had been nothing like this, she thought blindly as Travis's demanding kiss brought her to heights of passion and excitement she hadn't known existed. As Travis finally had to drag his mouth from hers and gasp for air, his voice was shaky and nearly angry as he growled low in her ear.

"When you are interested in your partner, you let him know. Not by pushing him away, but by moving closer for another kiss."

"Like this?" Wendy asked breathlessly, pushing ever closer to the fire that radiated from his hard body. Winding her arms around his neck, she searched for and finally found his mouth, bringing it back to hers.

Suddenly it didn't matter that she didn't know what she was doing. It didn't matter that she wasn't an expert in physical relationships with men. She knew human nature, and she knew that Travis wanted her kiss as much as she wanted his. Maybe she wasn't the most talented woman he'd ever kissed, or been kissed by, as she was doing now. But there was something alive, nearly palpable, that sparked between them every time they touched this way.

He bent her head back, and Wendy could feel his desire beginning to flare out of control right there in the middle of his driveway. Arching toward him, she threaded her fingers through his hair and moaned his name against his lips.

"Travis," she whispered, her voice husky against the dark. *"Teach me..."*

As though someone had tossed a bucket of cold water on him, Travis stilled, pulling back. "No," he groaned, taking a wobbly step away from the warmth of their embrace.

Dazed, Wendy looked up at him. "No, what?" Was he serious? They were just getting to the best part of the lesson here.

"No," Travis rasped. "We're never going to meet your goal if we keep this up." A raging fire burned in his eyes and he raked a hand across his jaw.

Again, he seemed almost angry. But why? Wendy just didn't get it. If anyone should be mad here, it should be her, she thought, watching as he turned, kicking his hacksaw and pruning shears out of the middle of the driveway, and strode rapidly toward his house.

"Hey," she called, suddenly ticked off herself. "What's the problem? Why are you so mad?" She rushed after him. He wasn't going to kiss her that way and then stalk off like a bratty little kid, packing up his toys and going home.

"I'm not mad," he flung over his shoulder. "It's late. You should be in bed." Turning, he scorched her with his burning gaze. "You have to get your beauty rest for the next guy on your list, right?"

Scurrying up his front steps, Wendy raced after him into his house.

"Travis, I don't know why you're acting this way. I'm sorry if I let you down with Abner there, but—" She threw his front door closed behind her and followed him into his living room. Standing in his path as he paced, she planted her hands on her hips and glared up at him. "Hey, I can't help it. The guy does nothing for me."

Reaching up, Travis massaged the tightly corded muscles in his neck. He hated himself for the perverse pleasure he took in knowing that Wendy still hadn't found her dream man. It was almost as if he wanted her to fail. But why? Was it for Dusty's sake? That's what he'd like to believe. But as he stood there, looking at her, her face flushed with displeasure, her chest heaving with anger, her eyes glittering with frustration, and her lips... rosy red and swollen from his kiss, he knew the reasons went far deeper than that.

He buried his face in his hands and rubbed his eyes. Geez. What a mess. Why couldn't things just go back to the way they were? Why did she have to go and spoil everything by embarking on this ridiculous husband hunt? He longed for the days when he and Dusty had her all to themselves. Life was so easy back then. So uncomplicated.

Then again, had it really been as wonderful as he'd like to remember? He'd been getting pretty tired of BambiAnn and the singles scene. If anyone could understand the humdrum life of a single person, he could. Lifting his bleary eyes out of his hands, he trained his gaze on her as she stood, her chin tilted defiantly at him, questions he couldn't answer burning furiously in her eyes. Oh, Lord, she was beautiful. Why was it, he wondered in confusion, that if he was truly so tired of the single life himself, he couldn't support Wendy in her efforts to leave it behind, as well?

The answer to that one was as complex as it was frightening, and Travis didn't want to have to delve too deeply into those waters. Last time he'd begun to feel this way about a woman, he'd ended up married to her. And, ultimately, abandoned by her. Not that Wendy was anything like Elly Mae. Anybody with half a brain could see that.

But, good grief, he wasn't ready to contemplate marriage again. And Wendy wanted a husband and a baby more than anything. Therein lay the crux of his problem. She wanted something he just wasn't ready to give. Not yet anyway. And as much as he wasn't ready to commit to her, he couldn't stand the thought of her making a life with another man. With other children.

Grinding his teeth, he felt about to explode with frustration. Crimeney damn. Someone else was going to get her.

Heavy bands of doom tightened around his heart, constricting his breathing.

Travis stared at her as she stood mere feet away, his eyes dropping to the mouth that spelled ecstasy for him. He shouldn't have kissed her again tonight. He'd known that, even as he was hauling her into his arms. This whole thing was killing him. Deep in his subconscious, he knew that the sooner she found a man and began her new life, the sooner he could get on with his. It was the only way. He simply wasn't as ready as she was to commit, and given her state of mind, he couldn't ask her to wait.

"I'm sorry about Abner." His voice was tight with emotion.

Wendy dropped her hands and slapped her thighs. "You should be." She sighed and, like an aging party balloon, floated tiredly onto his sofa.

"He was that bad?" he asked, sinking down at the opposite end, where it was safe.

Grabbing one of his throw pillows, she pulled it across her middle and tucked her feet up under her. She felt less vulnerable to him in this position. Sternly, she pursed her lips and her nod was curt. "Travis, Abner is a very sweet, very sensitive man. Extremely sensitive. We talked about his sensitive nature in great depth tonight. He carries the weight of the world on his shoulders."

"Are you sure he doesn't carry it in his belly?" Travis asked, a mischievous grin playing at the corners of his mouth.

"Very funny." Wendy sighed. "No. Do you know that Abner feels that it's his fault when it rains? He feels it's his fault when the Cowboys lose. It's his fault when his favorite TV show gets canceled. It's even his fault when the Fourth of July lands on a Wednesday and no one gets a three-day weekend."

"So that's who's responsible," Travis mused, a twinkle in his eye.

"Abner finds solace in food, Travis. Great mountains of food. And, being as he's such a sensitive guy—for crying out loud, he gets misty over the Clucky Fried Chicken ads—I couldn't point out to him that he eats like a pig. I mean, there was food everywhere! On his face, on his clothes, on *my* clothes, for heaven's sake. He belches and picks his teeth with the steak knife. He talks with his mouth full, not to mention *cries* with his mouth full. And he knows every fast-food joint in the entire state."

"I wonder if he's been to that new rib joint out on I-30..."

"Travis! This isn't funny!"

"Sorry."

"You know, I don't have to be in love with my future husband. At least, not right off the bat. And I made an honest effort tonight, when it came to kissing him. Maybe it wouldn't have been so bad if he hadn't eaten corn on the cob," she mused thoughtfully. "I just couldn't get past all those fuzzy teeth smiling at me that way." She shook her head ruefully. "Anyway, I may not have to be in love, but if I'm ever going to have my baby, I can't be repulsed by him."

Travis's eyes strayed to her flat belly and wondered possessively what it would be like to know that she carried his son or daughter beneath her breast. A smaller version of Dusty. His heart picked up speed and his breathing and blood pressure reacted not so subtly to the possibilities. The things she did to him—even from clear across the sofa, even though they were nowhere near touching—made him ache for her. Gave him a raw yearning deep in his gut to hold her the way she needed to be held her first time. To teach her the rest of the story when it came to making love. But, he couldn't. He wasn't ready for marriage. And for Wendy, he would settle for nothing less.

It was time to find her a husband.

* * *

"Dusty?"

"What?"

"C'mere, will ya?" Travis called from the kitchen where he stood next to the microwave, nuking their frozen dinners the following Thursday.

It had been almost a whole long, grueling week since Wendy's date with Abner. And in that time she'd gone out every evening with some Joe or another. That didn't even count the breakfast and lunch dates she managed to squeeze in, as she energetically interviewed her prospective husband candidates.

Popping open the microwave, Travis prodded the contents with a fork. Not done. Sprawling across the countertop, he reprogrammed his microwave and contemplated life at the post office with Wendy. Working in such close proximity with her while she executed her latest plan of attack on the husband hunt was one of the hardest things he'd ever had to endure. If he didn't wind up the post office remodel pretty soon, he'd go ballistic and wind up on the wall—in the form of a Wanted poster.

As it was, he'd given up his own dating life and practically turned into a damned monk, just so that he could keep tabs on the monster he'd created. A babe in the woods like her needed somebody to watch over them. He was the self-appointed guy for the job. Besides, BambiAnn and the crowd down at Little Joe's had completely lost their appeal. In fact, next to Wendy, they were positively dull.

Leaning over his drainboard, Travis squinted across his yard toward her place. She had another date tonight and he was trying to catch a glimpse of her as she moved around inside her house, preparing for her evening out. It was futile though. No matter how he craned his neck out the kitchen window, he couldn't see a blasted thing.

All day long she'd been very closemouthed about her plans for this evening. Refused to tell him who she was seeing tonight. The curiosity was driving him up the wall. He'd pretty much made an idiot out of himself, quizzing her. Pretending he wasn't jealous as he pumped her for information. But she wouldn't budge. Said she wanted to handle her love life her own way from now on.

That's what worried him.

"What, Dad?" Dusty padded into the room, his feet bare, his clothes mismatched, his hair sticking up on one side and looking as if it was filled with something... maybe jam.

The kid needed a mother, he thought shamefacedly as the timer on his microwave sounded. "Sit down, kiddo, dinner's ready."

Dusty frowned dubiously and sniffed the air. "What is it?"

"Fish sticks." He scratched his head. "I think," he said, tossing the steaming container onto the kitchen table and pouring them each a glass of milk.

"Yuck," Dusty complained when his dad dumped a pile of the stinky, mushy brown sticks onto his plate. "This isn't the way Wendy makes them. Wendy puts them in the oven. Then, Wendy makes French fries and tartar sauce." He poked at the lumpy pile with a wary finger. "Wendy wouldn't make me eat this, Dad."

"Well, Wendy isn't here, is she?" Travis snapped, squirting a glob of catsup over Dusty's fish sticks, hoping to disguise them.

Dusty was silent for a moment, then, chin tucked to chest, he muttered, "No. She's goin' out on a date tonight with some guy."

"Did she say who?" Travis asked quickly, hating the *of the* as he quizzed his son for information on the woman next door. "...o?"

"Yeah."

Travis leaned

"Reggie

Travis froze. *"Reggie Reno?"* he whispered and, leaping to his feet, ran to the living room window, just in time to see Wendy and Reggie pull away from the curb in his tricked-out, spiffed-up, cherry-condition, custom-designed van, complete with minibar, ceiling mirrors, big-screen TV and waterbed. The damn thing was a rolling hotel room and everyone in New Hope knew it. Everyone, it seemed, with the unfortunate exception of Wendy.

For a moment Travis contemplated grabbing his shotgun and tearing out after them, but ... who would take care of Dusty while he was out kickin' Reggie Reno's flashy butt? *Aw, Wendy. For pity's sake. What the devil are you thinking?*

Taking the opportunity to escape his less than palatable fare, Dusty ambled up beside his dad and stared out the window with him. "Neat van," the child observed as Reggie rounded the corner of the cul-de-sac, tires squealing, stereo blaring. Travis could feel the speakers vibrate from where he stood a block away.

"Yeah." Travis glanced worriedly down at his son.

"Dad?"

"Hmm?" Travis asked distractedly as his eyes surveyed the empty street.

"I don't think Wendy loves Reggie."

Smiling, Travis reached out and ruffled Dusty's hair. "What makes you say that?"

"Because I think she loves us."

He took a deep breath and carefully regarded his son. "I know she loves you, anyway, Sport-o."

Wide-eyed, Dusty looked up at his father. "You, too, cou. I can tell. Why don't you guys get married? Then she Out my mom. I think she wants to."

icy tentacle uths of babes, Travis thought absently. The thawed somew He wis ion that had grabbed hold of his heart were true. He wis 's innocent words. He wished it 't so hell-bent on finding a husband. He wished he had more time to explore the possibilities. But, wishing wouldn't make it so. It was good that she was getting on with her life. He just wished it wasn't with the oily Reggie Reno.

"Hey, buddy, what say you and me go get us a burger? Those fish sticks are rank."

"Yippee!" Dusty jumped up and down. "We can go to World of Burgers!"

"Why there?"

"'Cuz that's where Wendy's goin'."

Travis felt a wide grin split his face. "World of Burgers it is, buddy. Go put your shoes on."

The following Monday at noon, Wendy dusted off a sawhorse and sank gratefully onto its rough, less than comfortable surface. Surveying the work Travis was doing in her back room at the post office, she smiled with satisfaction. He was good. The best. She was so glad that he'd won the bid on this job. Without exception, he was giving her everything she wanted, and more. The craftsmanship was superb, the job was winding up in a timely manner and Travis looked wonderful in a tool belt.

Was that why he'd crept into her dreams on a nightly basis, ever since he'd been working at the post office? she wondered, inhaling the scent of sawdust and drywall and coffee and after-shave. She loved these smells. Try as she might, she couldn't seem to get them out of her mind at the end of each day. And it was only getting worse. The harder she tried to forget the effect he had on her—his kisses, the way he smelled, the way he looked in a tool belt—the more he haunted her dreams. Her daydreams were no exception.

The sad thing was, she was making an honest effort to be attracted to each of her dates. To give them the benefit of the doubt. But each weeknight date she went on, each post office patron she flirted with, each breakfast and lunch date endured, only further proved to her that there was no man out there who compared to Travis Donovan.

"Lunchtime?" Travis queried, glancing at her as he carried a sheet of plywood across the room and set it against the wall.

"Yeah," Wendy said, making her way to the small refrigerator and retrieving her brown bag.

"What, no lunch date?" Travis feigned shock.

"Not today. I needed a breather. Besides," she said, wagging a finger at him as she took her seat at the break table, "I'm afraid you and Dusty would only show up to stare at me the whole time."

"Can't." Travis shrugged easily as he pulled his own lunch out of the refrigerator. "Dusty's in school." His smile was mischievous. "So, how'd it go Thursday night, once Dusty and I left World of Burgers?"

Wendy tossed her hair over her shoulder and snorted in a most unladylike fashion. "Well, it's safe to say that I crossed Reggie off my list."

"Why's that?" Travis wanted to know, joining her at the table and digging through his lunch sack.

Crossing her eyes, she stuck out her tongue. "The man has a vocabulary that would send a concrete wall up in flames."

"That bad, huh?"

"Only every other word was bleeping this and bleeping that. Can you see me married to this guy? Having children with him?" Leaning back, she stared at the newly textured and painted ceiling for a moment, then dropped her gaze to Travis. "I can just hear the bedtime stories. Cinde-bleeping-rella and her bleeping stepsisters..."

Travis laughed as giddy relief swept through him. Good. Another one bites the dust.

"You know," she confided offhandedly as she reached into her bag for her apple, "I tried all your kissing tips on

Reggie. And on some of the other guys I went out with this week, as well.''

Travis stopped chewing his sandwich and stared at her. She had? "Oh?" he asked in a tightly controlled voice, and tried to swallow the suddenly dry wad of bread that had lodged in his throat.

"Yeah," she continued, taking a thoughtful bite of her apple.

He watched as the juice ran down her chin. What would she do to him if he leaned across the table and tasted that juice? With a valiant effort, he managed to swallow.

Wiping her chin on her paper napkin, she regarded him under the heavy fringe of her lashes. A look of hopelessness flashed across her face. "I don't know what's wrong with me, Travis. I just don't feel anything. I've tried everything you taught me and...nothing." She looked plaintively at him.

"I, uh, don't know what to say," he said, mentally cheering. So. The earth had yet to move when it came to kissing another man. *Yes!* He gave himself a mental high five, and tried to look appropriately sorry for her. With any luck, she would give up on this cockamamy husband hunt.

"I think it must be me," she lamented. "They can't all be that bad."

"No," Travis hastened to reassure her, "it's not you."

"How do you know?"

"I know."

Unable to sustain eye contact, Wendy abruptly changed the subject. "Travis?"

"Hmm?"

"Larry Miller is coming over for dinner in two weeks— he's going out of town for the holiday and won't be back till that Monday morning and I want to make something special. I have a new recipe, and I was wondering if I could try it out on you and Dusty this Saturday night."

Larry Miller? He groaned inwardly. Where did she dig up these losers? he wondered, closing his eyes so that she couldn't see him roll them at the ceiling. Larry was a regular down at Little Joe's. As far as Travis could see, he didn't have many redeeming qualities at all, unless you counted his astonishing ability to mix a martini in his mouth.

A wave of protectiveness threatened to bowl him over, and it was everything he could do not to demand that she cancel her date with Larry.

However, it was none of his business. Maybe she saw something in Larry that he had missed. Maybe he would be the one. He sighed. Suddenly he'd lost his appetite.

"It's nothing too fancy. Just a recipe I found in the *Metropolitan* magazine," she explained, eyeing the conflicting emotions at war on his face.

"Sure. We don't have anything planned." Unless, of course, she counted the hours he would spend sneaking from window to window, spying on her.

"Great. Seven o'clock, okay?"

"We'll be there."

10

"That new recipe of yours is a winner," Travis said, patting his full stomach through his oversize gray sweatshirt. He lay sprawled out on Wendy's living room floor, his shoulders and head propped against the sofa on several of her decorative pillows. They'd cleared away the last of the dinner dishes, laughing and talking and teasing as they worked together. Dusty played underfoot until his bedtime, then after a bath and a story, he hit the hay in Wendy's spare bedroom. He loved to spend the night with her and referred to the room as his.

It was the third Saturday in November, and it was chilly out. A cheerful fire crackled and popped in the fireplace, and as Wendy came into the room carrying a tray, she smiled down at Travis. Joining him on the floor, she turned toward the relaxing heat and handed him a cup of coffee.

"So, you think Larry will like it?" she asked, referring to the meal they'd just consumed. She pushed the large, blousey sleeves of her soft pink angora sweater up on her arms and took a sip from her own cup.

"Um," Travis nodded, staring into the fire. "I think he'll love it." Unfortunately, he lamented to himself. His hands balled into two involuntary fists. Who wouldn't love the whole package? A smart and beautiful woman. A great cook. A cozy home. A super conversationalist. A sexy as all get-out kisser. He shifted uncomfortably, in an effort to quell the unruly image of Wendy and him getting all hot and bothered out in his driveway the other night. She'd better not kiss old Larry. Not that way. He didn't trust old Larry as far as he could throw his truck against a stiff wind.

He took a deep breath and let it out slowly. Yeah, he thought sourly, somebody was going to win the jackpot when it came to marrying Wendy. She had a lot of great qualities. Not to mention the one thing he liked best about her. The fact that she didn't watch soap operas.

He shifted his gaze from the fire to her gamine features, outlined in the ethereal glow of the flames. The pink of her sweater brought out the roses in her cheeks, and her eyes sparkled with intelligence and health. She was so relaxing and easy to be with. But at the same time, she could drive him wild with excitement. He knew the kisses they'd shared were only the tip of the iceberg when it came to a physical union with her.

What would it be like to be married to Wendy? he wondered as a small fantasy of happy domesticity played in his mind. Travis really didn't know for sure. His own marriage had only lasted a year, and that had been to a woman who spent the days of her life living in another world. He didn't have much to base his ideas about marriage on. It wasn't as if his folks had set any example. They had divorced when he was younger than Dusty. However, he could imagine that marriage to someone like Wendy could be real nice. His eyes swept over her mouth. Nicer than nice. He wanted to pulverize Larry.

"The Russo wedding is November 28, this coming Saturday afternoon, one week from today," Wendy murmured, her own gaze fastened, unseeing, on the flames.

"Wow." Travis was surprised. It seemed like they'd just celebrated Halloween. These last few weeks had flown by.

"Mmm-hmm." Wendy nodded slowly, mesmerized by the occasional swirling sparks as they headed up the chimney.

"Doesn't look like I'm going to be attending on the arm of my fiancé." Her tone was crestfallen.

"I don't know about that." Travis shrugged easily in an effort to cheer her flagging spirits. "Once Larry gets a load of your new recipe..." He cringed, hoping that Larry would choke on her new recipe.

"It won't matter," Wendy sighed and, blinking, refocused her eyes on Travis. "My date with Larry is Monday evening, two days after the Russo wedding. And, the day after that, I turn thirty."

"Oh." Travis couldn't help it. He was glad she wouldn't be engaged by her thirtieth birthday. Unless Larry lost his mind over her new dish and proposed on the spot. No, that probably wouldn't happen, and he was relieved. He wasn't ready for her to announce her engagement. He needed more time to adjust. Plus, it wasn't as if she'd have to go to the Russo wedding alone. Heck, these days half the male population of New Hope would be only too happy to escort her. "Why don't you go to the wedding with Dusty and me?" he suddenly heard himself ask, knowing that, for him, it was the only solution. It was the only thing that felt right—the three of them, going as a unit.

Wendy thought for a moment, then smiled broadly. "That would be fun." Bringing her legs up under her, she leaned forward, elbows on her faded, blue-jeans-clad knees, toward Travis. "It wasn't the splashy entrance I'd hoped to make, you know, with a big old diamond and all. But I think I'll end up having a better time with you two."

This proclamation pleased Travis to no end. "Well, good, then. It's a date." He held his cup up to her before taking a sip.

Following suit, Wendy spoke across the top of her mug. "Have you gotten a wedding gift for Michael and Michelle yet?"

Sending her a blank stare, Travis shook his head. "No. I've been busy." Keeping tabs on the wild woman next door took a great deal of his time and energy. Besides, he never knew what to do in these situations. He knew about power tools and trucks. He doubted that a new drill would make an appropriate gift in Michelle's opinion. Which reminded him. He was going to have to pick out something for Wendy's thirtieth birthday. Something special. "In fact, I forgot all about it," he admitted sheepishly.

"Me, too," Wendy sighed. She shifted her position to lean back against the sofa next to him. Tilting her head, she gazed thoughtfully up at him. "Maybe we should go in on something together."

He returned her gaze. The warm glow of the fire in the dim and shadowy room had him relaxed and mellow, lying there with her. He never wanted to move again. "Sounds good to me. Why don't you pick out something, and I'll give you whatever you need, money-wise."

"Okay." Wendy smiled drowsily. "I think I'll pop in on Faith, down at the Baby Boutique and see what she's giving them. Maybe she'll know what Sue Ellen and Beth are getting, too. That way we can avoid getting them too many toasters, and the like."

"Good idea," Travis agreed companionably. She was so smart. And sexy. If he wasn't so full and warm and comfortable and worried about how she'd react, he'd be tempted to haul her across his chest and kiss about ten years off her life. That would solve both their problems.

Reaching behind his head, he pulled Wendy's wool throw off her sofa, and into his lap where he unfolded it and spread it over both of them. Then he propped his pillow under his head and, moving closer to her, shifted Wendy onto her side and pulled her into the curve of his body, spoon-style. There, he thought, feeling the exquisite sensation of her warm, soft body snuggled against his, and the heat of the fire toasting their toes. *Now* he never wanted to move again. "That's better," he murmured.

"Mmm," Wendy agreed, and he could see her cheek lift with her smile of contentment. "What are you and Dusty doing for Thanksgiving?"

"When is it again?" Travis asked, his eyes drifting shut.

"This Thursday. The twenty-sixth."

His eyes shot open. "Oh, yeah?" Man. He really had lost all track of time. All due to the little woman he held in his arms.

"Yep." Wendy nodded. "I take it you don't have any plans?"

"No." He'd probably just defrost something for him and Dusty. Something with turkey in it.

"Neither do I. I spoke with my folks on the phone yesterday and they're going to be out of town with friends for the next two weeks. And my sister Wanda is spending the holiday with her latest boyfriend, in the Caribbean."

"I'm sorry." Travis could feel her light shrug against his chest. It pained him that her family seemed to forget about her this way. They seemed secure in the knowledge that Wendy was self-sufficient. Could take care of herself. That might be true, he thought protectively, but it didn't mean that she didn't have feelings, too. As long as he'd known Wendy, something had always come up at the last minute for her family during the holidays. It seemed that, with the exception of Dusty, she spent many special days by herself. Must be why she was so anxious to marry and start that family. So she wouldn't be alone.

"No big deal," she said, then added, "since you guys don't have any plans, why don't I make us a turkey? We could spend the day together. Watch a little football on TV."

That sounded like heaven to him. "Okay. Great." Travis was surprised she hadn't already lined up several potential husbands for a trial holiday run. Not that he was complaining. Far be it from him to suggest this to her. Not when it meant home cooking for him and his boy. Not when it meant spending the day with the woman they loved.

Aw, man, he thought, closing his eyes, disgusted with himself. It was time for him to head home. When he started thinking this way, he needed a cold shower and a hard right cross to the jaw.

The soft pink glow of the lights that illuminated the Baby Boutique beckoned Wendy as she scurried down the sidewalk on her lunch break the following Wednesday. Someday, she thought longingly as she peered into the window at the sweet, attractive displays that Faith had so meticulously arranged. Someday, she would be coming to the Baby Boutique to pick out things for a baby of her own.

Though, at the moment, that possibility seemed about as likely as winning the lottery. Sometimes the emptiness in her heart threatened to consume her. Nothing, it seemed to Wendy, could fill the void but a husband and a child to call her own.

In a way, she envied Faith. Not the part about being a single parent, she mused, knowing that Faith had her work cut out for her, but the part about having a soft, warm, fuzzy little bundle to sing to and rock and hold...

The whisper-soft bell announced Wendy's presence as she moved out of the chilly wind and into the warm haven of motherhood. A quick glance around told her that Faith must be in the back. A small smile tugged at her mouth as she examined the small velvet-and-satin Christmas dresses for baby girls.

"Oh," she murmured, trying to picture her own baby girl in something like the white eyelet and green velvet dress that drew her touch. A little girl with soft blond hair. Like Dusty's. And fathomless gray eyes. Like Travis's.

"Faith," she called out to her friend. "These little dresses are adorable. Listen, honey, I know you're busy so I won't keep you," Wendy said, moving through the wonderland of baby fashion. "I just stopped by to find out what everyone got Michael and Michelle for their wedding, so that I can figure out what to do. I know it's last minute and every-thing, but Travis and I have been so busy and, well, to be honest, it just slipped ... our.... Faith?''

At the low sniffing and crying sounds that seemed to be coming from behind the counter, Wendy paused and lis-tened. Faith? Something was wrong. Was she in trouble? Was it the baby? *Oh, no!* Her pulse roaring in her ears, Wendy quickly strode toward the anguished moans. Wasn't Faith's due date any minute now? Wendy tried to mentally calculate, but fear froze her brain.

"Faith?" she called, worry crowding unbidden into her throat. Rounding a large shelving group of toys she found her friend staring bleary-eyed at what looked like the Russo wedding invitation. "Faith?" she breathed, "are you okay?"

Faith's smile was watery. "Oh, hi, Wendy." Trying to af-fect an airy laugh, she only succeeded in hiccuping. "I'm fine." She waved a delicate hand and the light tissue from the invitation rustled in the breeze she created. "Really. I guess I'm just a little misty." Again, she attempted laugh-ter. "Weddings do that to me."

Nodding, Wendy followed her back out to the middle of the store. "I know. Me, too," she admitted for Faith's ben-efit. It must be rough for Faith, she thought sympatheti-cally, having to watch Michael and Michelle's happiness as they embarked upon their lives together, when the father of her unborn baby was nowhere in the picture.

The bell over the front door rang softly again and Faith quickly wiped at her eyes with the back of her hand. "I'll be right with you," she called over her shoulder without look-ing, and smiled at Wendy.

Her smile faded as a male voice responded. "No hurry. I just need directions to the formal-wear place."

Faith's cheeks drained of blood, leaving a whitish pallor where there had been a healthy glow only a moment be-fore. Wendy stared at her friend in concern. *Oh, no,* she thought, looking around for a chair for Faith. Wendy couldn't be sure, but it looked like Faith was going to faint. Good gracious, she thought, her mind whirling frantically. She was no paramedic. This pregnancy business was downright scary.

Faith reached out and clutched Wendy's arm as she slowly turned to face her latest customer. *Ah, no, Faith,* Wendy moaned inwardly. *Forget the customer. You're in no shape to wait on anyone.* Her eyes cast quickly about for an adult-size chair but, to her eternal chagrin, landed only on the pint-size version.

The handsome customer—who Wendy recognized as Nick Russo, brother of the Russo groom—took a step toward them and smiled uncertainly as Faith loosened her grip on Wendy's arm and slid slowly to the floor.

"Ohmagosh," Wendy squeaked as her hands flew to her face in consternation. "I had a feeling this was going to happen." Glancing quickly up at Michael Russo's brother, she dropped to her knees and took Faith's wrist in her hand. "Nick, right?"

"Yes," he nodded, quickly stripping off his leather jacket and coming to her aid.

Wendy looked up into his capable, reassuring eyes, and suddenly felt less afraid. Something told her that he was the kind of guy a person could lean on in a pinch. Glancing helplessly down at Faith, she said, "Her pulse is strong, and she seems to be breathing all right. Do you think we should call 911?"

Reaching out, Nick placed a gentle hand on Faith's forehead, smoothing back her hair. "Mmm." He shook his head slightly. "I think she just fainted. Why don't we get her to a more comfortable resting place and then call her doctor?"

"Good idea," Wendy agreed. "There's a couch in the back."

As easily as if Faith had been a small child, Nick lifted her limp form into his arms and carried her to the office in the back. While he settled her on the couch, Wendy grabbed the phone, called the hospital maternity ward, and asked them to page Lucas Kincaid, Faith's doctor. As they waited for the return call, Nick helped Wendy elevate Faith's feet and bathed her face with a damp cloth.

"Have we met?" Nick asked, glancing up at Wendy as she hovered over his shoulder, handing him fresh cloths.

Wendy nodded. "Last February. At your brother's engagement party." She held out her hand. "I'm Wendy Wilcox, a good friend of Faith's." She glanced down at the still unconscious woman who was beginning to stir slightly. "And, uh...your brother and his fiancée's."

Taking her hand in his, Nick's brows formed a contemplative line. "I'm sorry. I'm a little fuzzy on that night." His smile was sardonic. "Had a little bit too much of the punch, I guess."

"You're not the only one," Wendy said, remembering how Travis had had to pull the lampshade off BambiAnn's head on more than one occasion that evening.

The phone rang, and Nick spoke to Faith's doctor. Faith began to rouse, drawing Wendy's attention. Once Nick was sure that Faith was in good hands, he bid Wendy good afternoon, donned his leather jacket, and took off without directions to the formal-wear place he'd been looking for.

Odd, Wendy mused, watching his retreating back as he disappeared into the crowd out on the street.

"Wha-what happened?" Faith stammered groggily.

"You fainted, honey." Wendy smiled and patted her hand. "But the doctor says you're going to be just fine. He wants to see you, though—"

"Is he still here?" Faith interrupted, a sudden note of panic in her voice as she struggled to sit up.

"The doctor? No, we spoke to him on the phone while you were sleeping."

"No," Faith moaned, nearly frantic with frustration. "Nick. Is Nick still here?"

"Nooo..." Wendy frowned, wondering what to do. Should she run after Nick? Why Faith should be so anxious to see Nick in the first place was beyond her. Risking her health—and the health of her unborn baby—Wendy's gaze shot to Faith's stricken face.

Faith had fainted at the sight of Nick Russo. Wendy counted backward to the last week in February. Faith had hosted an engagement party for Michael and Michelle. Nick was at that party. Then, Nick left town...

Wendy's eyes collided with Faith's.

"Yes," Faith moaned, and let her head drop back against the arm of the couch. "He's the father of my baby."

Unfortunately, Wendy thought as she basted the plump, succulent turkey that emitted such fabulous smells from her kitchen, Faith had sworn her to secrecy. She was dying to rush into the living room, where Travis sat with Dusty watching football, and blurt out the truth. The juicy truth that she—and she alone—knew.

Nick Russo was the father of Faith's unborn baby.

Wow. The burden of secrecy was killing her, and she'd only known for twenty-four hours. What must it be doing to Faith? This put a whole new spin on the Russo wedding for her. Would Faith attend? Did Nick know? Did the rest of the Russo family? Would they end up together?

All in good time, she sighed, closing the oven door and wiping her hands on her apron. A wedding was most certainly not the time or place for a revelation such as that to occur, so most likely, like the rest of New Hope, she would just have to wait and see.

"Halftime," Travis murmured into her ear as he came up behind her, grabbed her around the waist and growled into her neck. "What smells so heavenly in here?" he asked, peering over her shoulder at the stove.

For a moment Wendy allowed herself to melt back into his virile, sexy, utterly masculine body and imagine that he was her husband. Closing her eyes, she smiled. The image was so wonderful. It was so sad, how she'd gone and fallen in love with the wrong man, smack-dab in the middle of her husband hunt.

Her eyes popped open and she stiffened. It was true. That's exactly what she'd done. She'd fallen in love with Travis. A low moan sounded deep in her throat. What an idiot. Would she forever be a day late and a dollar short?

"Mmm." Travis buried his nose in the tender spot between her neck and her shoulder. "I love that little noise you make," he said, planting a few small kisses. "Ah. I think I just found out what's so delicious," he teased, tightening his grip at her slender waist. "It's you."

Luckily, before Wendy could angle her mouth back to his for one of those hot, zingy kisses that threatened to straighten her perm, Dusty wandered into the kitchen.

"Is it ready yet?" he asked, sniffing around, much like his father.

Travis dropped his arms. "Is it?" he whispered teasingly, trailing his hand down along the gentle swell of her hip.

Wendy's eyes shot to his. "It's getting there," she said, and reveled in the smoldering look that flashed across his face.

"Oh, man," he groaned, his eyes sweeping roguishly over her curves. "Dusty," he ordered, grabbing his son by the arm, "let's set the table. I'm starving."

Wendy grinned. Yes, but starving for what? As she covertly watched Travis direct the table setting procedures, she couldn't help but notice once again what a wonderful, loving father he made. Just the kind of father she wanted for her own baby someday.

A lump formed in her throat as she admitted that it was never to be. Travis had been too badly hurt by Elly Mae, and could probably never give his heart to a woman again. As much as she understood this, it didn't make her situation any easier. Darn it, anyway. His kisses had ruined her for any other man.

She should know. Lately she'd kissed her share of toads. Perhaps nearly as many as the social butterfly, BambiAnn. Heaving a heartfelt sigh, she checked the turkey one last time. How the heck was she supposed to lure a man into the marriage trap, if her heart was still with Dusty's daddy?

Later that evening, after they'd all claimed that they were fair to bursting, and Dusty had trundled off to bed, Travis watched Wendy as she gathered the table linens in a laundry basket and put the crystal back into her china cabinet. There was no getting around it anymore. He was in love with Wendy Wilcox. And now that he'd finally come to his senses, it was too late. She was on a mission, and Larry Miller was her latest target. He might as well forget the notion that she might aim Cupid's bow at him. No. In her mind, he was a lost cause. Not that he blamed her. He'd failed in the husband category before.

She saw him as a womanizing playboy. To a degree, she'd been right. But, dang it, anyway, a man can change. Crimeney, if someone had asked him a month ago if he'd be thinking about tying the knot now, he'd have died laughing. And if they'd asked him if he'd be thinking about tying it with Wendy, he'd have just plain died. But here he was, mooning over her like a lovesick bull, wanting nothing more than to marry her and make babies with her.

She and Elly Mae couldn't be any less alike if they tried, in all the ways that counted. He could see that now, and knew that he could trust Wendy with his life. More important, he could trust her with Dusty's life. She was serious, loving, good-natured, well liked by the community and smart. Not to mention sexy as hell when she was just being herself and not wearing the hideous postal uniform or the garish big hair and makeup. She even seemed happy with her life here in New Hope, content to settle down and leave the wanderlust to the people on the soaps. He'd blown it. Should have staked his claim when he had the chance. Viciously punching his pillow, he stuffed it behind his head and settled in to wait for Wendy to come join him.

At long last Wendy finished her chores, and brought their customary pot of coffee out to the living room. Settling next to him on the floor again, she smiled contentedly, purring like a kitten when he took her legs into his hands and began rubbing her calves.

"Mmm," she said, closing her eyes. "I'll give you exactly fifty years to stop that."

"Deal," Travis said solemnly, and meant it.

"I got Michael and Michelle a wedding gift yesterday," she murmured lightly.

"Yeah?"

"Yeah. I went to the Baby Boutique to ask Faith what everyone else was doing, but . . . she was with a customer."

"Oh. So, what did you decide on?" he asked, working his thumbs into the back of her knee.

She giggled. "That tickles."

"Sorry."

"No. Don't stop," she ordered. "I like it." Closing her eyes again, she pursed her lips. "Let's see . . . where were we?"

Travis knew where he'd like to be. It was everything he could do not to drag her into his arms and kiss those puckered lips. Man. Was she trying to kill him here? "You were, uh, telling me about what we bought for the Russo wedding."

"Ohhhh, yeah," she moaned, and he thought his chest would explode. "Uh, we bought them some silverware."

"Silverware?" Travis asked in a strangled voice.

"Yeah. Silver. They were registered for a really pretty pattern down at Monaco's Department Store. So I got several settings for them. It's gonna cost ya,'' she sang teasingly. ''I hope you don't mind.''

''That depends on the cost,'' Travis said, his voice loaded with innuendo.

Wendy grinned. ''I'll go easy on you.''

Allowing his head to loll back on his shoulders, Travis exhaled wearily at the ceiling. Impossible. There was nothing remotely easy or simple about his relationship with Wendy.

11

Monday evening, the day before she turned thirty years old, Wendy looked into the mirror and saw a changed woman. And not because she was any closer to topping the crest of the dreaded hill. No. It went far deeper than that. She exuded a new maturity. A subtle grace. A certain loveliness that came only with hard won self-confidence.

If this husband hunt had been successful on any level at all, it was in the fact that it had forced her to grow up. To take a long, hard look at the path she was taking, and to alter her course for the better. To come out of her shell and meet the world face-on. And, most important, to allow herself to become vulnerable to another person.

Although, a fat lot of good it did, she thought morosely as she styled her hair into the sleek chignon she'd copied from the latest copy of *Metropolitan*. So now she was filled with confidence and poise. So what? She still couldn't have the man she wanted. Needed. Ached for. Dreamt about by night, couldn't stop thinking about by day.

Story of her life. She sighed and nervously dabbed a little perfume behind her ears. Any minute now Larry Miller would be showing up at her door and the whole exhausting getting-to-know-you process would begin again. For the millionth time, she desperately wished that she could marry Travis. She already knew him. She already liked him. More than that, she already loved him and his son to distraction.

Oh, Travis, she thought, her heart heavy with sorrow. Why did she have to look any farther than the end of her driveway for the other half of her heart?

But as much as she longed for a relationship with Travis, it wasn't to be. Travis had no intention of ever trusting again. Of ever loving again. Of ever marrying again. He'd been hurt too badly. Besides, she wasn't his type. And no matter how hard she tried to alter her appearance and her behavior, she never would be. She just couldn't sustain the dumb-blonde routine. At heart, she was just an average woman who wanted the simple things in life.

A nice guy like Travis and a few kids to call her own.

Moving to her closet, she slipped her new, stylish black-and-white polka-dot-print dress over her head. The silky material floated down and clung becomingly to her figure. She cinched the wide belt at her narrow waist, deep in thought. What a mess she'd made for herself.

Not only was she in love with Travis, but she needed him. As much as she knew he needed her. As much as Dusty needed her. Heavens, they were practically a family already. That's the way everyone had treated them, at the Russo wedding. Just like a family. She'd loved the feeling of arriving at the sanctuary on Travis's arm, taking her place on the pew between him and Dusty. Watching Michelle and Michael take their vows of love together. He'd held her hand, squeezing it from time to time, and it had all felt so right. It all made perfect sense. Too bad Travis would never see it that way. Oh, well, she thought, wiping at a stray tear that blurred her vision. It was too late anyway.

Travis was afraid of marriage.

Tomorrow she would be thirty.

Larry was on his way.

Snatching a tissue from her nightstand, she blew her nose and, taking a stoic breath, crossed the room to her dresser. She didn't even particularly like Larry, she mused morosely as she fastened her new black-and-white earrings into her ears and slipped her pumps onto her feet. It hadn't been her idea to have him over for dinner. Someone down at the post office had told him about her husband hunt, and he'd invited himself over. Just like that.

Coating her lips in a bright, rosy shade of lipstick helped boost her confidence a little. She looked nice enough for the questionable Larry, she decided, powdering her nose and checking her stockings. Her heart just wasn't in this date. They'd have a little dinner together and—unless he was really able to impress her in some way or another and change the niggling feelings of doubt she had about his character—she would most likely start the whole process over again next weekend with someone else.

Except that, by next weekend, she would already be thirty. And her chances of landing that man, according to the article anyway, were practically nil. A sudden headache gripped her brain and she longed to take a couple of aspirin and crawl into bed. To hide from the world. That way, she could just skip the whole depressing ordeal with Larry. Deep in her soul, she knew that they were all wrong for each other. Just as she had known about Abner and Reggie and the host of other suitors she'd considered.

Staring at herself in the mirror, she gave her head a little shake. Since when had she become so picky?

Since she'd started comparing every man she met to Travis, she guessed wryly. Without exception, they all came up short next to him.

It was funny, but in the past month he'd changed nearly as much as she had. A small, sad smile tinged the corners of her mouth. He probably didn't even realize it, but he hadn't been out on a date with anyone but her since BambiAnn had left him for Cecil. In fact, he'd even admitted that he was ready to stop acting like a wounded animal and start taking responsibility for his and Dusty's future. Amazing. Neither of them was the same person at all anymore.

The fading twilight drew her inexorably to her bedroom window, where she leaned against the sash and gazed into Travis's yard. Somehow, she must have sensed his presence because he was standing there in his drive, arms crossed firmly across his powerful chest, legs spread slightly for balance, his brow furrowed in concentration as he pondered a seemingly heavy thought. Wendy's sigh was haunted. He was everything she'd always wanted in a man. Why hadn't she ever been able to see that before?

She'd always liked Travis, just the way he was. But now...now she was in love with him. Probably always would be, until her last, dying breath.

Someday, when she and her husband were old and gray and sitting out on the front porch in their matching rocking chairs, she would probably look next door toward Travis's place with the same hollow yearning she felt for him right now.

The doorbell chimed, interrupting her ruminations. Larry was here. Taking a deep breath, she dragged her eyes from the man she loved, cast a last-minute glance over her appearance, then headed to the door to let Larry in.

Larry had arrived.

Time to go prune Wendy's side of the hedge, Travis thought grimly, grabbing his gardening shears and hacksaw as he headed toward her yard. He pondered the idea of bringing his shotgun, but thought better of it. Might not need it on the hedge, but then again, you never knew...

He squinted at Larry's beater, parked at the curb in front of Wendy's place. Something about that guy bugged the hell out of him. He couldn't quite put his finger on it, but he wasn't about to let Wendy serve that loser dinner, alone in her house, without keeping an eye on the both of them.

Burning off his nervous energy, he attacked the hedge with a renewed vengeance. Most likely, when he was done with the poor thing, there would be nothing left. He paused in his assault. Was he thinking about the hedge, or Larry? Didn't matter. Sweat broke out on his brow as he worked and strained to see something through Wendy's picture window.

Anything.

Damn.

Nothing.

Couldn't hear anything, either. What was going on in there? he wondered, whacking savagely at the leafy green.

"What are ya doin', Dad?" Dusty asked as he ambled up behind his father. His soft, baby-fat belly was peeking from beneath the sweatshirt he'd outgrown.

"What does it look like?" he barked, then immediately felt like an old ogre. He shouldn't take his frustration over Wendy's idiotic love life out on his son. He should be taking it out on her. Dagnabbit, anyway. What the devil was wrong with him? Why didn't he just march himself over there and claim her as his woman and get it over with? He wanted Wendy. She wanted a husband. Dusty wanted a mother. They all wanted each other. It had become amazingly clear in his mind. "I'm pruning the hedge," he explained in a softer tone and smiled at his curious son as he mopped his brow.

"In the dark?"

"It's not totally dark yet."

"The streetlights are on." Dusty pointed up.

"Yeah, well." Travis lifted and dropped his shoulders, then stared over at Wendy's picture window. The curtains were drawn. Why had she drawn the curtains? She never did that. Probably just so she could drive him crazy. Well, he thought discontentedly, it was working.

"You know what I want for Christmas, Dad?" Dusty asked, picking up his father's hacksaw and swinging it around in wild circles.

"Dusty, you're going to put somebody's eye out with that thing," he admonished and, never taking his gaze off Wendy's window, reached out and took the saw.

"Do ya, Dad?"

"Do I what?"

"Know what I want for Christmas?"

"No."

"I want Wendy to be my mom."

"That's nice." Travis nodded absently, wishing he could be a fly on the wall over at Wendy's place. What the hell was going on over there, anyway? The not knowing was killing him. How could he drop by and check things out, without seeming obvious?

"And so you're gonna hafta ask her to marry ya pretty soon."

"Mmm," Travis hummed as his eyes scanned the various windows at her house. Perhaps he could just wander over and take a little listen. If nothing was wrong, he'd just go back to trimming the hedge.

"You could get married on Christmas," Dusty continued, warming to his plan. "I wouldn't want any more presents than that," he promised solemnly.

"Rightttt," Travis exhaled the word slowly as he thought. Dusty was right. It was getting dark. No one would notice if he did a quick perimeter check of her property. No big deal. Maybe she left the drapes open at the other side of the house.

"So, you're gonna do it?"

"Yep." Travis nodded with determination. Military maneuvers from his National Guard days swam in his head. That's just what he'd do. He'd protect her from another of her less than suitable suitors one last time. After tonight, there would be no next time. After tonight, Wendy would be his. Permanently. End of story. No more of this wacky husband hunting plan of hers. She already had a husband for the taking. Him. He grinned broadly. Damn. It felt good to have that decided.

"Yeah!" Dusty cried, jumping into the pile of laurel branches that lay in the middle of the driveway and spinning with joy.

Travis's gaze shot to his jubilant son. What on earth was that all about? he wondered as he watched his happily cavorting son. Whatever it was, Dusty was on cloud nine. He smiled fondly at the boy. He loved to see him so happy like this. He'd do anything to keep that look of sheer, unadulterated rapture on his sweet, baby face.

"Listen, kiddo," Travis said, still grinning. "I've got a few things I've got to do out here. Why don't you go get ready for bed, and I'll be in after a while to check on you."

"Okay!" Dusty shouted with unaccustomed good nature. Rarely did he capitulate so easily when it came to getting ready for bed. As he tripped and skipped across the yard and up the stairs to the front door, Travis heard him singsong, "Wendy's gonna be my mom on Christmas! Wendy's gonna be my mom on Christmas!"

Where the heck did he get that idea? Travis wondered, scratching his jaw. Heading over to Wendy's yard, he ducked low and, glancing around to make sure no one was watching, proceeded to sneak into her backyard in hopes of getting a glimpse of... well, something.

Larry had been drinking.

That much was obvious. Wendy stood in the kitchen, wringing her hands and fussing as long as she dared with her new recipe. The new recipe that Travis loved so much. *Oh, Travis.* She sent a frantic, silent plea for help in his direction. *Help.*

"Can I do anything to help?" Larry's voice, rough and slurred and filled with disgusting innuendo, reached her from where he sat impatiently waiting in her dining room.

"No, everything's ready," she chirped nervously. What would he do to her if she asked him to leave? Probably wouldn't take too kindly to it, she decided. Oh, how she wished this evening was over. Maybe she wasn't as worldly as she liked to think she was these days, because she didn't have a clue as to what she should do with this man. This man she'd taken a sudden and intense disliking to.

Travis would know what to do. Travis would take care of everything. If only Travis were here. Of all the days for him to decide to stop spying on her, she thought, agitated. For weeks now he'd been sneaking around, watching her every move. He thought she hadn't noticed. But she had. And where it had irritated her before, now she would kill for a glimpse of those curious gray eyes.

Taking a deep breath, Wendy picked up her casserole dish, pasted a smile on her face and headed out to the dining room. If she was lucky, maybe Larry would pass out in his plate and she could call a cab to take him home.

As she caught sight of his craggy, leather-yellow complexion, his greasy, thinning hair, his stooped-over posture and his soiled and wrinkled clothes, there was one thing she knew for sure. There was no way in hell she was going to kiss this toad. The husband hunt was officially over. If she couldn't have Travis, she didn't want anybody. Especially not a sleazebag like Larry.

Breezing to the table, she set her dish down and tucked a serving spoon next to it.

Larry peered at the dish, his lip curling with disdain, then swung his leering gaze up to her.

"Help yourself, Larry," she urged, trying to still her shaking hands. "I'm just going to go get us...some—"

"Don't mind fie do," Larry slurred, cutting her off as he bared his crooked yellow teeth at her and pulled himself to his wobbling feet. Lurching wildly against the table, Larry inadvertently tilted and cleared the table of her entire afternoon's labors.

She stared in shock as her clear glass casserole dish bounced off the wall, sending Travis's favorite dish splattering across the floor. The rest of the table accessories, the centerpiece, the salt and pepper shakers, the long, tapered candles, spun and rolled crazily across the hardwood. Wendy's heart leapt to her throat and lodged there, cutting off her supply of oxygen. Paralyzed with fear, she stared at him as he staggered toward her.

"Oops." He burped, stupidly thumbing his handiwork. "Don't worry about a thing. We'll jusss clean thad up later. But firsss, how 'bout a li'l kiss for ol' Larry, huh, sugar?"

Wendy gave a quick, rapid shake of her head. "No," she whispered.

"Oh, c'mon now, sugarlips, I know you're lookin' for Mr. Right, and—" he pounded triumphantly on his hollow chest, then reached out and grabbed her arm "—I'm here to apply for the job. So, pucker up, baby, and less get this show on the road." His gurgly laugh was raspy from years of smoking his own hand-rolled cigarettes.

"No, thank you, uh, Larry," Wendy squeaked, trying to wrench out of his grasp.

"Ah, a little hellcat. I like that," Larry rasped woozily, then belched again. "Ya know, Wednesday, everybody in town's sayin' what a looker you are these days. So I'm thinkin' to myself, Larry old boy, she's the one you've been waitin' for. Come to Papa, honey doll." His yellow lips loomed at her, puckered and gaping like a dying carp.

His nauseating breath filled her nostrils, sickening her. She was going to faint. No, she was going to vomit. No, she was going to scream.

No.

She was going to beat the stew out of this...this... *scumbag,* she thought, taking aim and letting him have it where it counted with her knee. As he stumbled back toward the wall, shock and pain causing his eyes to bulge in a most satisfying manner, Wendy pulled back and let him have it in the nose with her fist, screaming like a banshee all the while.

She would never be able to remember exactly what happened next. She only knew that shortly after Travis came crashing through her back door, she found herself sitting in a dining room chair watching as he knocked Larry cold with one swift punch to the jaw.

Bounding easily over Larry's inert frame, Travis rushed to Wendy's side and swept her into his arms. "Are you all right?" he breathed, his voice cracking with emotion as he pulled her into the living room, away from the mess and the drunken lecher who'd caused it. Once there, he crushed her to his chest where his heartbeat echoed in her ear and, cradling her head against his shoulder, murmured noises of comfort.

Wendy nodded mutely, her eyes squeezed tightly shut against tears of relief and stood trembling like an autumn leaf. "Oh, Travis," she sobbed. "Thank God, you're here. I didn't know what I was going to do."

He sighed and a low, rueful chuckle rumbled in his throat. "Looks to me like you were doing a pretty good job of handling the situation," he praised, admiration tingeing his voice along with something Wendy couldn't identify. Something that sounded vaguely like possessiveness. "I don't think I've ever been so afraid," he admitted. "When I heard you scream, I thought I was gonna have a heart attack." He tightened his hold on her. "I don't know what I'd have done if that creep had hurt you." His jaw worked convulsively against her temple.

Crystal teardrops spiked her lashes as she looked up at him through the dim light that filtered from the hall. "Where were you?" She sniffed plaintively. "What took you so long, anyway?"

An uncertain frown tugged at Travis's brow. "I'm not sure I know what you're getting at."

Wendy's smile was soft. "Oh, come on, Travis. I know you've been spying on me for weeks now."

His grin was sheepish. "You knew?"

"You were pretty obvious." She exhaled tiredly. "You'll be happy to know that you can hang up your magnifying glass, spy boy," she informed him, nestling into the comforting crook of his arms.

"I can?"

"Yes." She nodded. "The husband hunt is officially off. As of midnight tonight, I'll be thirty, so..." She took a deep breath and shrugged haplessly. "I lose." Darting a quick glance up at him, she smiled wryly. "No big deal."

Feeling suddenly weak in the knees, Travis sank to her couch, pulling her alongside him. The husband hunt was off.

The husband hunt was off!

Wait a minute. Did that mean she didn't want a husband anymore? His heart sank like a bowling ball in a swimming pool as his mind whirled with the ramifications.

Okay. She didn't want to get married. At least he and Dusty would have no more competition for her affection. For a while, anyway.

Although, how long could that last? he wondered, his eyes straying out to where Larry still lay sprawled out on her dining room floor. If he didn't make his move now, sooner or later she would be back in the middle of the dating scene and eventually hook that husband. And in the meantime, how was he supposed to keep his sanity?

There was no way in hell he could take another episode like the one he'd just had to live through. Worrying about her safety, worrying about her having to leave Dusty and concentrate on her own family, worrying about her sharing her kisses with another man, worrying about how he could face the coming years without her companionship... Hell, he was even worrying about how much he'd be worrying.

Nope, he decided grimly. She couldn't give up on the idea of marriage yet. Not before he'd had a chance to propose.

He was going to propose whether she liked it or not. A sense of exhilaration so powerful it nearly knocked him out of his work boots swept over him. He was ready. *He was ready!* He drank in the poignant sight of her sweet, tear-streaked face as she nestled against his shoulder. It was so clear. They belonged together. They were made for each other.

What could the single life possibly have to offer him that a life as Wendy's husband and lover couldn't? Nothing, he thought vehemently. Not a blasted thing.

He stroked the soft hair at the top of her head. And they could have that baby. Soon. A little brother or sister for Dusty. Yeah, he thought, studying her velvety brown eyes as she dabbed the tears from her splotchy cheeks with a black-and-white polka-dotted sleeve. A little baby that looked just like her. He'd like to get started on that right away. In fact, he couldn't think of a single thing in his entire life that he'd rather do.

"Wendy?"

"Hmm?" She sighed deeply and angling her head slightly back, smiled a watery smile up at him.

"Did the article say you had to be married before you were thirty, or just engaged before you were thirty?" he asked, shifting in his seat slightly so that he could face her. Reaching out, he took her hand in his.

"Um..." She stared absently at their hands, locked together so comfortably. "I think it said being engaged was okay, as long as an official date was set. You know, so that the engagement doesn't become an excuse for not getting married." The steady tick-tock of her mantel clock drew her eyes. "Not that I have to worry about that anymore," she said with a small, stilted laugh. Wendy threw a quick glance over her shoulder at Larry, who had begun to snore peacefully beneath her table, a bit of her new recipe curdling beneath his onerous breath. "I only have a few hours left before I'm officially over the hill."

Travis tipped her chin up with his thumb. "Hey," he teased, "it's not so bad on the other side. I'm here."

Wendy's gaze clung to his. That was a nice thought. It made the downhill slide a tad more tolerable.

"Besides," he continued, "if you wanted to, you could be engaged by your thirtieth birthday." He looked at her with a curious mixture of uncertainty and hope.

A sharp laugh squeaked past Wendy's lips. "No, thank you," she demurred, casting another disillusioned glance over at the slumbering Larry.

"Would you decline my proposal, then?"

Wendy's head spun back around to Travis, her heart beginning to pound beneath her breast. What was he talking about? "What proposal?"

"Marriage." A light flared in his eyes as he took her hands in his and placed them flat against his heart. "Will you marry me, Wendy Wilcox?" As if suddenly nervous, Travis touched his tongue to his lower lip and ran his palms back and forth over her wrists.

Stunned, she glanced around the room, as if he could be speaking to another Wendy Wilcox. One that he loved. One that he wanted to marry. "Me?" she whispered, barely daring to believe. Travis Donovan, diehard single, was proposing to her? Light-headed, she blinked up at him. He wanted to marry her?

"Yes. You." His liquid gray eyes swept tenderly over her face. "The way I see it, you need a husband and Dusty needs a mother. And..." Pausing, he tightened his grip on her hands. "Sweetheart, I need you. I can't stand the idea of losing you to another man." His eyes narrowed as he darted a disgusted glance in Larry's direction. "And since I've fallen head over heels in love with you, getting married just seems like the natural thing to do.''

Her jaw went slightly slack as she tried to digest this latest turn of events. Could she be dreaming? No, she mused as Larry snorted loudly and rolled onto his back. This wasn't exactly the romantic setting of her dreams, but the result was the same.

Travis was in love with her, she thought, her breath catching with sudden wild excitement in her throat. *He loved her! How wonderful!* He knew every boring, embarrassing detail of her simple life, yet he wanted to sign up for a lifetime. With her.

''I'd like to set a date, right now, too.'' His smile dimpled down at her. ''That is, if you're willing?''

Eyes flashing, she searched his face. ''Could, you . . . uh, say th-that again?'' she stammered, weak with delirious delight.

Travis grinned. ''I'd like to set a date?''

''No.'' She shook her head, clutching his hands, feeling the erratic pounding of his heartbeat as he pressed them to his chest. ''The part before that.''

''It just seems like the natural thing to do?'' he teased.

''No, no, no!'' she cried gleefully. ''You know what I mean.''

''I'm hopelessly in love with you,'' he said solemnly as the embers of hope and love flared to life in his eyes. He brushed his lips lightly across hers. ''I may not have always realized what it was we've had all these years together,'' he murmured, ''but, Wendy, ever since you moved in next door, I've been busy tangling my life with yours. Depending on you for everything from someone to laugh and talk with to someone to give my son a much needed mother's touch. It just took nearly losing you to someone else for me to see it.''

''I can't believe it,'' she whispered in awe.

Travis frowned slightly, puzzled. "Why?"

"Because I love you, too."

"You do?" The lines between his eyes eased and a wide smile transformed his handsome face. "Why didn't you say something?" he breathed as relief shuddered through him.

"Because you were so down on marriage. And I wanted a family. A little boy just like Dusty, and a husband to love, just like you. But..." She sighed. "I didn't think you'd ever consider me."

Travis laughed. "I've been driving myself crazy, thinking the same thing. I didn't think you could see me as the marrying kind." He passed a hand over his jaw. "After all, I've loved and lost before."

"Better than never loving at all," Wendy said ruefully. Taking his cheeks between her palms, Wendy drew his face down to hers for a kiss that was a promise of the joys to come. "We're quite a pair," she murmured, smiling against his lips.

"Mmm," he agreed, and pulled back slightly to look deeply into her eyes. "So. Will you marry me?"

Tenderly, she traced the curve of his mouth with her fingertips. "Yes," she whispered. "I'll marry you."

"Yeah!" The joyous shriek came from Wendy's entry hall. Dusty burst out from behind the front archway where he'd been hiding ever since he'd heard his dad crash through Wendy's back door. "On Christmas, right, Dad?"

Travis shrugged loosely and arched an eyebrow at the woman both he and his son loved so dearly. "You got any plans for Christmas?"

Beaming, Wendy gave her head a slight shake and tugged Dustin onto her lap. "Looks like I'll be getting married."

"All right!" Dustin crowed, wriggling happily.

"Happy birthday," Travis whispered over his son's head, and kissed Wendy softly on the lips.

"The happiest," Wendy murmured, eagerly returning his one of a kind kiss.

Larry snored contentedly in agreement.

* * * * *

Don't miss the next book
in Silhouette's exciting
DADDY KNOWS LAST series.

Here's a sneak preview of

DISCOVERED: DADDY

by Marilyn Pappano

available in November from
Silhouette Intimate Moments

Discovered: Daddy

Faith Harper ignored the chair behind the counter and paced restlessly around the shop. It was the day before Thanksgiving, and the store was quiet. She had planned on going home early but it was five-fifteen, only fifteen minutes before her regular closing time, and Faith was still there. She'd done the usual closing-up chores and now all she had to do was flip over the sign on the door from Open to Closed, shut off the lights, lock up and leave.

Still she waited.

She thought, believed, *hoped* he would come—if not to the shop, then to her house. But just in case he chose the shop, she had to stay until closing time. She had to give him every minute of opportunity.

He. Him. Nick Russo.

With a sigh, Faith glanced at her watch. Five twenty-five. Maybe she'd been wrong in thinking Nick would prefer a meeting here at the shop—maybe he would prefer the privacy of her house. Maybe he wouldn't come at all. Maybe...

The bell rang, and she went cold inside. It was him. She didn't have to turn to face the door to know it. She could feel it. The door closed and slowly, gathering her courage, she turned to face him. He stood, hands in his jacket pockets, shoulders squared, his expression not quite a scowl. Grateful for the racks of clothing between them, Faith clasped her hands together underneath her belly, her way of connecting with Amelia Rose, of reassuring her daughter that everything would be all right.

For a time, they simply looked at each other. Finally he broke the silence. "How are you?" The question was grudgingly polite, the concern minimal, the sincerity nonexistent.

"I'm fine." She sounded no friendlier, not even as polite.

With a vague nod, he glanced around the shop. Checking to make sure they were alone? she wondered. Was he afraid of someone seeing him there? More than likely, his wife wouldn't be easily put off by the knowledge. She would wonder what business Nick, the tough-guy cop, might have in a baby shop.

Faith would love to tell her...but, of course, she wouldn't. Except for blurting out her secret in this afternoon's weak moment to Wendy, she'd told no one. Not one other soul in town knew, or even suspected, that Nick Russo was the father of her baby.

He moved a few steps closer. Taking up a position directly in front of her, he glanced away, then back again. Like that, his antagonism disappeared and was replaced with bewilderment. "Who are you?"

For a moment she simply stared at him, then she became aware of a sinking sensation in her stomach. "I expected better from you than that," she said flatly. "If we weren't alone, if somebody else were around to hear... But we are alone. There's no one else here."

"I know your name is Faith—the woman earlier told me that. Have we met?"

Made restless by her disillusionment, Faith turned and walked to the counter. "I knew I would see you this week. I knew you'd come back for Michael and Michelle's wedding. I even knew you wouldn't be too pleased by what you saw. But I never imagined that you would be so cowardly as to pretend not to know me."

"Lady, if I knew you, I wouldn't be here," Nick said sharply. "I only came back because..." Breaking off, he grimaced. "Apparently, you think we've met before. Pardon me for not remembering, but when was it?"

"We met at your brother's engagement party." Her voice was soft, her words as cold as the ice inside her.

"Michael's engagement party?" He shook his head. "I don't remember...."

"Oh, please," she said scornfully.

"Look, I admit, I got drunk that night. There's not a whole lot about it that I do remember. Did something happen? Is that why you're acting this way?"

She studied him for a long time, searching for some evidence of his deceit. Once again she found nothing. He looked confused, curious, a little chagrined by his admission of drunkenness and a whole lot blank. He wasn't playing a game. He wasn't pretending.

He didn't remember her!

FORTUNE'S Children™

Bestselling Author

BARBARA BOSWELL

Continues the twelve-book series—FORTUNE'S CHILDREN—
in **October 1996** with Book Four

STAND-IN BRIDE

When Fortune Company executive Michael Fortune needed help
warding off female admirers after being named one of the ten most
eligible bachelors in the United States, he turned to his faithful
assistant, Julia Chandler. Julia agreed to a pretend engagement, but
what starts as a charade produces an unexpected Fortune heir....

MEET THE FORTUNES—a family whose legacy is greater than riches.
Because where there's a will...there's a *wedding!*

"Ms. Boswell is one of those rare treasures who combines humor
and romance into sheer magic."
                                                                 —*Rave Reviews*

A CASTING CALL TO
ALL FORTUNE'S CHILDREN FANS!
If you are truly one of the fortunate
you may win a trip to
Los Angeles to audition for
Wheel of Fortune®. Look for
details in all retail Fortune's Children titles!

WHEEL OF FORTUNE is a registered trademark of Califon Productions, Inc.©
1996 Califon Productions, Inc. All Rights Reserved.

Look us up on-line at: http://www.romance.net   FC-4-C

Take 4 bestselling love stories FREE

Plus get a FREE surprise gift!

Special Limited-time Offer

Mail to Silhouette Reader Service™

3010 Walden Avenue
P.O. Box 1867
Buffalo, N.Y. 14269-1867

YES! Please send me 4 free Silhouette Yours Truly™ novels and my free surprise gift. Then send me 4 brand-new novels every other month, which I will receive months before they appear in bookstores. Bill me at the low price of $2.69 each plus 25¢ delivery and applicable sales tax, if any.* That's the complete price and a savings of over 10% off the cover prices—quite a bargain! I understand that accepting the books and gift places me under no obligation ever to buy any books. I can always return a shipment and cancel at any time. Even if I never buy another book from Silhouette, the 4 free books and the surprise gift are mine to keep forever.

201 BPA AZH2

Name	(PLEASE PRINT)	
Address		Apt. No.
City	State	Zip

This offer is limited to one order per household and not valid to present Silhouette Yours Truly™ subscribers. *Terms and prices are subject to change without notice. Sales tax applicable in N.Y.

USYRT-296   ©1996 Harlequin Enterprises Limited

As seen on TV!
Free Gift Offer

With a Free Gift proof-of-purchase from any Silhouette® book,
you can receive a beautiful cubic zirconia pendant.

This gorgeous marquise-shaped stone is a genuine cubic
zirconia—accented by an 18" gold tone necklace.

(Approximate retail value $19.95)

Send for yours today...
compliments of ▼ *Silhouette*®

To receive your free gift, a cubic zirconia pendant, send us one original proof-of-
purchase, photocopies not accepted, from the back of any Silhouette Romance™,
Silhouette Desire®, Silhouette Special Edition®, Silhouette Intimate Moments®
or Silhouette Yours Truly™ title available in August, September or October at your favorite
retail outlet, together with the Free Gift Certificate, plus a check or money order for
$1.65 U.S./$2.15 CAN. (do not send cash) to cover postage and handling, payable
to Silhouette Free Gift Offer. We will send you the specified gift. Allow 6 to 8 weeks for
delivery. Offer good until October 31, 1996 or while quantities last. Offer valid in the
U.S. and Canada only.

Free Gift Certificate

Name: _____

Address: _____

City: _____ State/Province: _____ Zip/Postal Code: _____

Mail this certificate, one proof-of-purchase and a check or money order for postage
and handling to: SILHOUETTE FREE GIFT OFFER 1996. In the U.S.: 3010 Walden
Avenue, P.O. Box 9077, Buffalo NY 14269-9077. In Canada: P.O. Box 613, Fort Erie,
Ontario L2Z 5X3.

FREE GIFT OFFER
084-KMD

ONE PROOF-OF-PURCHASE

To collect your fabulous FREE GIFT, a cubic zirconia pendant, you must include this
original proof-of-purchase for each gift with the properly completed Free Gift Certificate.

084-KMD

This October, be the first to read these wonderful authors as they make their dazzling debuts!

THE WEDDING KISS by Robin Wells
(Silhouette Romance #1185)
A reluctant bachelor rescues the woman he loves from the man she's about to marry—and turns into a willing groom himself!

THE SEX TEST by Patty Salier
(Silhouette Desire #1032)
A pretty professor learns there's more to making love than meets the eye when she takes lessons from a sexy stranger.

IN A FAMILY WAY by Julia Mozingo
(Special Edition #1062)
A woman without a past finds shelter in the arms of a handsome rancher. Can she trust him to protect her unborn child?

UNDER COVER OF THE NIGHT by Roberta Tobeck
(Intimate Moments #744)
A rugged government agent encounters the woman he has always loved. But past secrets could threaten their future.

DATELESS IN DALLAS by Samantha Carter
(Yours Truly)
A hapless reporter investigates how to find the perfect mate—and winds up falling for her handsome rival!

Don't miss the brightest stars of tomorrow!

Only from *Silhouette*®

Look us up on-line at: http://www.romance.net   WTW

You're About to Become a
Privileged Woman

Reap the rewards of fabulous free gifts and benefits with proofs-of-purchase from Silhouette and Harlequin books

Pages & Privileges™

It's our way of thanking you for buying our books at your favorite retail stores.

PROOF OF PURCHASE
Offer expires October 31, 1996
YT-PP186

**Harlequin and Silhouette—
the most privileged readers in the world!**

For more information about Harlequin and Silhouette's PAGES & PRIVILEGES program call the Pages & Privileges Benefits Desk: 1-503-794-2499

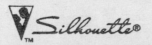

™

YT-PP186